THE HAND OF THE DEVIL

DEAN VINCENT CARTER

Delacorte Press

Published by Delacorte Press
an imprint of Random House Children's Books
a division of Random House, Inc.
New York

www.randomhouse.com/teens

Educators and librarians, for a variety of teaching tools,
visit us at www.randomhouse.com/teachers

Library of Congress Cataloging-in-Publication Data is available upon request.

The text of this book is set in 12-point Garamond.

Printed in the United States of America

10 9 8 7 6 5 4 3 2 1

First American Edition

For Mum and Dad . . . for everything

We live on a placid island of ignorance in the midst of black seas of infinity, and it was not meant that we should voyage far.

—*H. P. Lovecraft*

PROLOGUE

Zaire
2 July 1932

The old hut stood alone on the shore. Low mist from the water floated like a shroud across the sand, swirling around the small wooden structure before dissipating into the line of trees behind it. Cutter could hear the sound, even from his position several meters away. He wiped his brow with the damp rag from his pocket, then turned and nodded at his guide, Obi. They approached the hut slowly, hesitantly, only too conscious of what lurked within.

Obi stopped, inhaled deeply, then gave his charge a cautious glance. Cutter smiled before realizing with some alarm that his companion was trembling.

"You've been very brave to have come *this* far," he assured him. "Stay here. I'll go in alone." He put a hand on the man's shoulder.

"I can't move," Obi murmured, the shame unmistakable in his voice.

"Don't worry. I understand." Cutter turned and looked back at the hut. It would be a ghostly sight even without the graveyard mist from the river. Now the buzzing, the maddening cacophony, was playing tricks with his mind. He could swear that the small building was expanding, swelling in size from the noise building up within.

1

"If you call out," Obi said, his voice full of regret, "I may not come to your aid, my friend."

"I know," Cutter replied. "It's all right."

He continued forward, parting the fog with his feet, until he reached the wooden door. The sound was awful now. He tried hard to ignore it as he lifted his hand to the door handle. Going in would require a tremendous effort and at that moment he seemed to lack the necessary strength of will. His mind was hindering his body with visions of what awaited him on the other side of that door. He applied pressure to the handle. The door didn't move.

Cutter was consumed with the same paralyzing terror that had so stricken his guide. The Lady was in there, and she was waiting for him. This he knew beyond all doubt. He closed his eyes and ordered his body to push, to fight.

Somehow his hand moved as though guided by an unseen force and pushed down the handle. It took some effort, but the door eventually yielded. Voices were screaming inside his head, ordering him to stop, to turn away. He knew that the cold, sickening fear, coupled with lack of sleep, was feeding his already wild imagination, but he couldn't stop now. Even though he was closer to death than ever before, he couldn't turn back. She already had him in her grasp. He knew he should have returned to the village for assistance. He knew he should have kept his promise to his wife and steered clear of such danger. He knew a lot of things.

The crack between the old door and its warped frame

widened. At once the noise erupted from the dark confines of the hut, encompassing the man and disrupting all thought. He stood still, barely able to see anything inside the dim structure, but knowing all the while that she was there.

Obi still couldn't move. He was renowned among his people for his strength and courage, but that was before he'd learned that the monster was real. This was something he could never have prepared for. He had grown from boy to man with the legends of his tribe, but not until this day had he imagined that they held any truth. Seeing Cutter standing with his hand on the door of the hut, he knew. The terror on the white man's face was clear. It was in his eyes, in the pallor of his flesh. Something landed on Obi's upper lip, but he couldn't even blow it off. The white man was shaking now. He'd opened the door wide enough to step inside the hut.

The walls were alive. Cutter saw dark, ever-changing shapes smothering the sides of the hut. Waves, odd phantasms formed by thousands upon thousands of tiny, whining insects. An old bed frame and a wooden box were also covered in the creatures, leaving no patch of wood visible. Then he saw her, and his heart nearly stopped. On a crude shelf fashioned from a section of bark sat a huge red mosquito. In appearance she was not dissimilar to the millions of bodies around her, but her size was incredible. She was easily as large as a child's hand. Undisturbed by the frenzy of her followers or the arrival of the intruder, she just sat there, facing him.

Now, summoning more control over his body, he took a net and a large jar from the bag slung around his shoulder. After all the years he'd spent in the field, his tools remained simple, crude but effective. He unscrewed the top from the jar and slipped it into his pocket. The mosquitoes were now swarming over his shoes, some deciding to venture up his legs. He shuddered, nearly losing his grip on the jar. Raising the net above his head, he advanced toward the shelf, treading on countless tiny bodies, praying he wouldn't provoke a mass reaction. She seemed to be tracking him with her eyes, her wings lifting and lowering slowly. He readied himself to bring the net down, and that's when he heard the terrible shriek.

It seemed to be inside and outside of his head simultaneously. The bloodcurdling sound was like the agonized scream of a lunatic. The atmosphere changed within the hut: the dark patches on the wall dissolved, and thousands of small shapes took to the air, forming a thick cloud around him. The Lady remained silent and still. Cutter now realized that the scream he'd heard must have been a premonition: it was identical to the sound now tearing from his lungs.

After the Lady's followers had gorged themselves on the man's blood, it was her turn to feed. By the time she had finished there was little more than a drop of red fluid left in the deflated body.

From the shore, Obi heard the chilling cry. Once the screaming had stopped, sensation returned to his body, along with a feeling of sickening guilt. He stood there for some seconds, willing himself to turn and run. Then, as if from the air itself, came a voice. A female voice.

Come—do not be afraid. I don't wish to harm you. . . .

His jaw dropped. His breathing became irregular. He'd heard the words, but he couldn't believe them. Could the myth be a reality? Could the creature really enter the mind of a man? It was impossible. But he hadn't imagined it, there was no doubt about that. She had called out to him.

Well?

Something was pulling him toward the hut. He had no wish to approach it, but he felt compelled. He looked from the hut to the setting sun, then back again. He closed his eyes and pictured his home, his family. Even as he thought he was breaking free from the hold on him, his feet began moving him closer and closer to the hut. *Please,* he prayed, his eyes still closed. *Please let me go.* His hand, no longer his own, reached for the door handle. Inside her lair it felt cooler. He awaited her embrace, and all it promised.

Two miles downriver, Ernest Faraday sat in the shade, wiping sweat from the freckled folds of skin above his eyes. In Africa he enjoyed none of the comforts he was used to at home, and each day brought some new horror, some new discomfort. He loathed the oppressive heat; it felt as if he were being steamed alive. He'd dreamed, the night before, that he was trapped inside the spout of his grandmother's old teakettle, unable to escape the endless steam. Although it was early, the temperature was a constant distraction. He hated it here. Even in the shade he was in hell.

And from hell he watched the natives haul the supplies up the riverbank from a boat moored nearby. They moved like one large, segmented creature, chanting a low mantra as they worked. From somewhere behind Faraday came a voice. It was female, although as far as he knew there weren't any women in the area. The only ones he'd seen in weeks were all back at the village some miles away. He twisted round and peered into the darkness of the trees. Nothing. He turned, pushed the sweat sideways from each eyebrow with his thumb and continued supervising the activity on the beach. He was convinced the heat was making him hear things.

Burke and Pollard, Faraday's two assistants from his London office, were busy arguing over the quickest method of transporting the goods up the beach. Burke was nothing if not enthusiastic, gesturing wildly with his hands as he followed the bemused workers up and down the sand.

"Look here," he said, "they're in a nice, orderly chain. I fail to see any merit in—"

"They should be carrying the stuff in pairs," Pollard interrupted, proving yet again that he could never agree with his colleague. "In pairs they could carry twice—"

A dog started barking somewhere out of Faraday's view. It was Carruthers, Burke's Yorkshire terrier.

Pollard winced. "Can't you muzzle that filthy beast? You know what I think of dogs!"

"Well, it can hardly be any worse than what they think of you," Burke snapped.

Pollard held his tongue, merely shaking his head in distaste.

Faraday sighed. He looked forward to sunset and a brief respite from the terrible sun. Swatting an insect away from his face, he watched the overworked natives, wondering why they hadn't deserted him weeks ago. Something landed on the back of his neck, escaping his notice. One of the workers started shouting and waving his arms about as Carruthers began chewing part of the wide breeches he was wearing. Faraday swore, got to his feet and started walking down to the water.

"Burke! If you can't control—"

The mosquito clinging to his neck chose that moment to insert its feeding tube.

It felt as though someone had jabbed a long, ice-cold needle into his flesh. Then, as the long, long seconds passed, the pain escalated and Faraday started to jump about in terrible agitation. He slapped the back of his neck repeatedly in a desperate and futile attempt to remove whatever was causing the agony.

His yells attracted the attention of Burke and Pollard, who now looked on in obvious confusion.

"What on earth is he doing?" Burke turned and began walking toward his boss.

"I don't know, but at least he's got off his lazy backside for once," Pollard muttered, following behind. They approached their employer, unsure of what to do or say.

"What the devil's wrong, Mr. Faraday?" Pollard stopped, his mouth hanging open. Burke had seen it too.

Fastened to the back of Faraday's head was what appeared to be a mosquito, but its size was wrong. Very wrong. It was huge. The two men stepped back, openmouthed. Faraday was now making the most dreadful sounds, his suffering clearly immense. The workers had ceased all activity and were staring somberly at the white man, as though they'd witnessed such a spectacle before.

"For God's sake!" Faraday shrieked. "Get it off me! Get it—" He staggered around blindly, then fell backward onto the sand, his eyes bulging, limbs twitching. In seconds he was dead.

Burke and Pollard locked eyes, then stared in disbelief at the body. Faraday's skin was quickly turning green. As they watched, horrified, the grotesque insect, now maroon in color from all the blood it had consumed, crawled out from under the man's head, flew up onto his forehead and crouched there, regarding the two men. Steam was rising from Faraday's wound. As the two men watched, liquid began soaking into the sand around the dead man's head. Some of it was blood; the rest was something else.

"Oh, my Lord Jesus." Pollard started retching. Faraday's head, it seemed, was dissolving.

The wings buzzed momentarily to life, then stopped, then buzzed again. The creature rose into the air. Burke and Pollard were only vaguely aware of the dog barking as it bounded up the beach toward them. Without warning the monster flew straight at them. In his panic to flee, Burke stumbled and fell, cracking his head open on a sharp rock. The pain was terrible but short, as death came upon him swiftly. Pollard, following suit, tripped over Carruthers and hit the sand. Turning, swearing and scrabbling about, he glimpsed the insect's long sharp feeding tube instants before it plunged into him. The sound it made was only faint, but Pollard's cries traveled miles.

Carruthers sniffed around his master's head, whimpering. He couldn't accept that he was dead. The natives were gone. Some of the supplies they'd been carrying were left abandoned halfway up the shore; some were starting to float down the river. After Pollard had stopped screaming and Carruthers had stopped whimpering, there was silence, save for the sound of the water, and a faint whine.

I: PROPOSITION

London
September 2005

My name is Ashley Reeves and I'm extremely lucky to be alive.

It's one thing to be told a scary story, and quite another to be right in the middle of one. But that was where I found myself only a few days ago, and I'm worried that if I don't write down each and every detail of my horrifying experience on Aries Island, I may end up convincing myself that it was all fiction, the diseased imaginings of a young man on the brink of madness.

That I survived the ordeal is a mystery in itself, for I stared death in the face more than once. But perhaps the most worrying aspect of it all is what drove me to visit that island in the first place. I'm a journalist, and therefore naturally predisposed to pursue stories. But this story should have made me cautious right from the beginning, and I realized too late that I had let my ambition lead me into more trouble than I could handle.

This account is of an extraordinary creature. A creature so dangerous that if it had been able to reproduce, it could have wiped us all from the face of the earth.

Mosquitoes are just insects. Nothing more than tiny

biological machines. But they are also carriers. They communicate diseases like malaria, yellow fever, West Nile virus, dengue and encephalitis. Transmitting infection seems to be their primary function. Mankind is perhaps the herd that mosquitoes are destined to thin: millions of lives have been claimed by malaria alone. But mosquitoes don't know what they are doing. They don't know they are carrying terrible diseases. It would be an incredible thing indeed if a mosquito, or any insect, were capable of thought.

But one thing I'm reminded of time and time again is that Mother Nature loves a paradox.

I think many journalists must come to a point in their career when they think they've heard everything. I came to that point surprisingly early, with stories about three-headed pigs, blue sheep and talking plants; the only thing that shocked me was the audacity of the idiots behind them.

The magazine I work for, *Missing Link,* was launched a few years ago. My editor, Derek Jones, left a newspaper he'd been with for several years and started up *Link* on his own, to cash in on the public's fascination for all things "inexplicable."

The magazine has done very well, building up a pretty respectable readership. I came on board some months ago, fresh from college with a degree in journalism. But by then certain changes had already taken place at *Missing Link.* Derek had just sold the magazine but had decided to stay on as editor. The new owner was obsessed with credibility and wanted *Link* to focus more on oddities and freaks of nature, than on what he deemed "nonsense."

Out went the little green men and in came the flora and fauna. Soon we were rebranded a "science magazine," dedicated to the weird and the wonderful. For me it was an exciting time and I was keen to get into serious reporting.

Gradually, however, doubts crept in about exactly what I'd got myself into. I'd been aware for a long time that honesty and journalism could be a difficult marriage, but I was surprised by exactly how difficult it was. I had to accept that the distortion of facts was not merely commonplace but ever present. Gradually elements of the job lost their appeal, but one that didn't was Gina Newport, the magazine's star photographer. At twenty-two she was nearly a full year older than me, and I'd liked her, a lot, from the moment I laid eyes on her. But somehow I could never find the opportunity or guts to do anything about the way I felt. Such is life.

Last Monday, a day that now seems lost in the mists of time, was the day the letter from Reginald Mather arrived. It was a glorious early autumn day, so I decided to run to work, taking my favorite route along the canal. After I'd reached the office, I showered, dressed and went next door to the newsagent's to buy a carton of orange juice. Sitting behind my computer, I opened the juice and began sorting through the small pile of mail the office assistant had brought me. Mather's letter was at the bottom, and was the only one that didn't end up being filed in the trash.

The letter was brief, something that caught my attention

straightaway. Usually the lunatics who write in waste page after page of paper trying to convince me that they have an amazing story for the magazine. Mather's letter was businesslike, concise and therefore more credible.

Dear Mr. Reeves,

I have in my possession a specimen known as the "Ganges Red," a unique strain of the <u>Aedes aegypti</u> mosquito family and the only one of its kind. If you were to ask an expert about it, they would no doubt tell you that it does not exist.

I have enclosed a map that will help you find your way to Aries Island, located in the middle of Lake Languor. I own the only house on the island, so you should have no trouble finding me. A boat can be chartered from Tryst harbor. I know the harbormaster to be a very helpful fellow, and can assure you that his rates are most reasonable.

It would be splendid if you could come right away, though of course I understand that a journalist's schedule must be fairly tight. I regret that I have no telephone, so shall expect you at any time, or otherwise a letter to say that you cannot come.

I must ask for your discretion in this matter. I am keen to share my discovery with the world, but being a private man I need to

PROPOSITION

keep certain details to myself. Therefore I ask, if it is possible, that you should not divulge the specifics of this letter to a third party.

I have the honor to be, sir, your obedient servant,

Reginald C. Mather

I read it through a second time. Unlike most of the letters I received, it was intriguing. I had a hunch that Mather's claim was genuine, and that there could be an exciting story lurking behind it. At the very least it could mean a day out of the office. I read it again, then made up my mind to talk to Derek. I was about to go and see him when a scrunched-up ball of paper hit the back of my neck.

"Ow!"

"Hey, Ash." It was Gina. "What's happening?"

"Oh, I was just going to have a word with Derek about whether to follow this up or not." I held up the letter.

"Anything good?" She sat on the corner of my desk, her close proximity already making me nervous, and took the letter. While she read it I tried not to stare up at her face. Sometimes I thought she liked me too, but it was never clear if she liked me enough.

"Sounds good," she said, handing back the letter. "You should go."

15

"Yes. There's a chance he could be another crackpot, though."

"That's what makes it so interesting." She grinned.

"I don't know. Some of these people are dangerous."

"Don't be so paranoid. Besides, you should jump at the chance of a nice day out."

"I know. I just—"

"Where does this guy live, anyway?"

"It's, er . . ." I picked up the envelope and read out the address written on the back.

"The Lake District?" Gina's eyes lit up. "Oh, come on, how can you not go? If you don't, then I will."

I nodded. She had a point. I'd never been to the Lake District, but I'd always planned to visit.

"I suppose I should check out train times."

"You do that," Gina said, patting me on the back. She slipped off the desk and started to walk away.

"Right." I looked toward Derek's office to see if he was on the phone. "But listen," I called out to Gina's retreating back, "if he does turn out to be insane, I'm blaming you."

"Would I ever lead you astray?" She sat down at her desk and began leafing through a pile of photographs.

"No, I suppose not," I replied, getting to my feet. I went and knocked on Derek's door.

I might have known how he would react. He preferred the sort of story that could be researched and written in a couple of hours. This one was likely to take up the rest of that day and quite possibly the next. When I walked in he was looking out of the window, and seemed lost in thought.

"Hi, Derek."

"What? Oh," he said, turning to me. "Sorry. I was . . ."

"Are you OK?" I closed the door behind me.

"Yes, I'm fine. I'm just concerned about a friend of mine. We worked on a magazine together years ago. He's been missing since last week. It's a bit worrying."

"Oh, I hope he's all right."

"Yes, me too." He sat down behind his cluttered desk. "Anyway," he said, putting the matter aside, "what can I do for you?"

I showed him the letter. When he'd finished reading it he asked me a few questions about what sort of article I could make out of it. He often did this, just to make sure I was already thinking ahead. "Is it really worth the trip, though?"

I had the feeling that he'd already answered this question himself. Nevertheless, I tried to assure him of the story's potential.

"This guy," he said, his eyebrows arched in doubt, "he sounds like a scientist or something. Has he written in before?"

"Not to my knowledge, but he sounds like he's on the level, which is a nice change. He doesn't say what his profession is in the letter."

"Hmm. Well, if you want to do it, I guess it's OK."

"Great." I turned to leave.

Derek stood and went back over to the window. "But,"

he added, "even if it turns out to be another fool's errand, bring *something* back, OK?"

I looked at him for a few seconds, puzzled by what he'd said. "What do you mean, 'bring something back'?"

"You know—make sure the time isn't completely wasted. You should know by now that it's bad practice to return to the office empty-handed, Ashley. Take some photographs of something. Fake them if you have to—just get something we can use."

"You're not serious?" I wasn't sure if he was joking or not. It was hard to tell with Derek. "You're the one who's always moaning about hoaxers and time-wasters!"

"I despair," he said, shaking his head but smiling. "You're supposed to have an imagination."

"Imagination? What about integrity?"

He just laughed. "Integrity, my arse. Go on, get out of my sight."

"I will. Oh—wait," I added, turning back. "Speaking of pictures, could I borrow Gina if she isn't busy?"

"No, you can't. And don't think I don't know what you're up to."

"What do you mean? I'm not up to anything."

"Oh, come on, I'm not blind, for God's sake," he said, grinning mischievously. "Sorry, but I can't spare her at the moment. You'll have to take your own photographs." He sniggered as I left his office, and I couldn't help wondering who else knew about my crush on Gina.

It made little sense to hang around the office, so I quickly finished up an urgent article, then made a couple of phone calls to get train times for the journey. As I left the office I passed Gina, who was on the phone. She mouthed "Good luck" at me. I wished she'd been able to come too. At the very least she would have been good company.

As I waited at the bus stop, I wondered if I should have had a look on the Internet for information on the Ganges Red. Still, Mr. Mather was likely to be the best source of information, since he had the creature in his possession.

Back at the flat, I put all my work gear (notebooks, tape recorder, etc.) into a backpack along with my iPod and camera, and left home to catch the tube to Euston.

The station was busy as usual. I spent a good twenty minutes in a long line before buying a ticket for the 12:45 train to Windermere, where I would get a connection to Tryst. With a few minutes to spare I bought some sandwiches and a drink from a food stand, and a paperback from the bookshop. When the train finally arrived, twenty-five minutes late, I was irritated and hoped there would be no further delays.

I found a seat, and soon the train was thundering through the countryside north of London. Most of the other passengers were businesspeople, with some day-tripping families and teenagers making up the numbers. I started reading the book I'd bought, barely registering the train's passage through Watford, Milton Keynes and Rugby. The journey progressed without incident until, shortly after leaving Nuneaton, a signal failure added another half an hour onto our arrival time. It was becoming increasingly unlikely that I'd be able to get back to London before the last train left from Windermere. It wasn't the end of the world, but I just hoped the story was worth it or Derek wouldn't be too happy about the expenses bill. I put down my book and stared out of the window at endless fields, rivers and roads, punctuated occasionally by a small town or farm.

At some point I fell asleep, rocked gently into slumber by the rhythm of the train. When I woke up we were pulling into Preston. I sat up, took out my iPod and listened to music for the next hour until we arrived at Windermere shortly before half past four. I spent the short trip on the connecting train to Tryst thinking of everything I knew about mosquitoes, which was practically nothing.

As the train approached Tryst, the number of passengers in the dilapidated carriage dwindled, until only an elderly gentleman and myself remained. I stepped off the train and onto the platform, surprised by how much the temperature had dropped in so short a time. It seemed as though winter had arrived three months too soon.

Far above me was a wide bank of gray cloud that didn't appear to be moving. I walked into the ticket office and asked for directions to the harbor. The woman behind the window asked if I was going out onto the lake, and I told her I was. She gave me a strange look.

"Really?" she asked. "You've picked a pretty awful day for it, young man. It'll be pouring down any minute now.

And it's getting dark out there." She leaned forward in her chair so that she could see the station entrance through the side of the booth.

I followed her gaze and nodded. "Yes. Just my luck. Oh, by the way, when is the last train back to Windermere?"

"Last train to Windermere," she began, turning to flip through a large folder on her desk, "leaves at seven minutes past nine."

I looked at my watch. It was just after five-thirty. Time, as well as the weather, was now against me. It was feasible that I could do the story and just about get back to the station to catch the last train. But by then the last train from Windermere to Euston would have left anyway. I wouldn't be going back to London that night.

"You wouldn't happen to know of a bed-and-breakfast nearby, would you?"

"You could try the Rocklyn up the street. They're pretty good there."

"The what?"

"The Rocklyn Bluewater. It's owned by an old stage actress—or so she says. Nice lady, though. She'll probably have rooms available at this time of year."

"Right. Thank you."

I stood outside the station for a while. It was getting quite cold and the sky overhead was attracting more and more dark clouds. I sensed approaching rain in the air. Looking to my left, I saw the lake itself, which dominated the view in that direction. The road before me sloped down past shops and houses toward one side of the vast stretch of water. The woman at the ticket office hadn't told me where to find the harbor, but it didn't really matter: I could see a small wooden boardwalk at the bottom of the hill with a number of boats in the water nearby.

I met only a few people along the main street. Somewhere a dog barked, but apart from that there was little evidence of activity. The shops along the road were old and poorly maintained. They gave off an air of apathy, an absence of love. A weathered sign on the side of a boarded-up shoe shop read: THE SHAMBLES. I was amused by its accuracy.

To my right, not far away at the top of the hill, I could see a large building with a board outside that read:

THE ROCKLYN BLUEWATER GUEST HOUSE VISITORS WELCOME!

After entering the building I approached the reception desk and spoke to the proprietress herself, who was a small, thin, elderly lady in rather eccentric clothes and what appeared to be a blond wig.

"Oh, hello, young man! I'm Annie Rocklyn—very pleased to meet you!" Her overfriendly attitude caught me off guard a little, as did the remarkable amount of makeup she'd applied to her face. "Now, what can I do for you? All our rooms are fully furnished and—"

"If I could just book a room for tonight, that would be great. I'm visiting someone on the lake."

"Of course! You're in luck as we have a number of

rooms available at the moment. Er . . . did you say the lake?" Her smile dropped a little.

"Yes, I'm a journalist," I said, in an attempt to impress. "I'm visiting a Mr. Mather. He lives on the island. Do you know him?"

"Not personally. Well, no one does, really, dear. He doesn't come into town." She leaned forward conspiratorially. "Keeps himself to himself, if you know what I mean."

"I see. So, shall I check in now or wait until later? I should only be a couple of hours."

"I lock the door at eleven-thirty, but if you get here later, just knock—I'm usually up late. I have always been something of a night owl." She smiled, the abundance of lipstick around her mouth catching the light from the gaudy desk lamp that stood beside the guest book.

"Right. Thank you very much."

I turned to leave. As I walked out I could hear Annie Rocklyn following me across the foyer, calling out, "You're from London, aren't you? Did I mention I once trod the boards in the West End?"

"Really?" I asked, not wanting to ignore her. "Were you in anything I'd have heard of?"

"Run for Your Wife."

"Ah," I said, unsure what to say next. "Good stuff. . . . Well, thank you very much. I'd best be off, I suppose."

"Oh, of course. And you take care now! Those can be treacherous waters in weather like this."

"I will. Thanks again."

I walked briskly down to the harbor, nearly tripping

on one of the loose stones that lay strewn across the dirt slope above the lake. I saw a boardwalk and an office or cabin of some sort, so I approached and knocked on the door. There was a loud cough, then a muffled curse. The door opened.

Whether it was bad timing or whether he just hated interruptions I don't know, but the man clearly wasn't pleased to see me. He was short, overweight and limping slightly. His long gray hair was yellowing in places, exposing him as a dedicated smoker.

"Well," he began brusquely, one eye opened wider than the other, as he exhaled a long plume of smoke into the air. "What do you want?"

"Excuse me, but are you the harbor manager?"

"Master," he replied, without changing expression.

There was an awkward pause before I replied, "Sorry. Harbormaster."

"I am."

"Oh, great. Could I hire a boat to get across to the island, if that's possible?"

"The island, eh?" He looked me up and down and smirked, as though something had amused him, then limped over to a desk and opened a large logbook. He seemed to take a long time to find what he was looking for. Through a grimy window I could see the rain clouds bunching together over the lake and the town. They looked certain to open at any minute. It was as though they were waiting for me to get out on the water before unburdening themselves.

"Name?" He licked the end of a ballpoint pen and prepared to write.

"It's Reeves. Ashley Reeves."

"And what is it you need?" He started writing in what looked like an uncomfortable manner, his hand curled around the pen like a claw.

"Just something small and simple to get me to the island and back."

"I see. You'll need something pretty nippy then if you're wanting to miss that rain," he said, staring through the glass.

"Yes. Rain's no good."

"No, it ain't. Pretty odd you choosing to go boating this evening then, ain't it?"

"I beg your pardon?"

"Number six," he replied, ignoring me. He took something from a shelf above the desk, then went out of the door, sniffing as he went. I followed.

Outside it felt as though a huge lung had sucked most of the oxygen out of the air. I could hear the sound of wood scraping on wood as boats bobbed against the dock.

"Should have brought some spare clothes," I said to myself.

"Eh?" The old man looked bemused. He took a deep drag on the soggy cigarette that seemed to be a permanent fixture on his face.

"Sorry. I was just thinking aloud. Mental sewage."

He shook his head and turned away.

At the end of the boardwalk the harbormaster stepped down onto the rocks at the edge of a small beach. A sorry-looking boat had been dragged onto the shore and abandoned.

There was a loud rumble from above, and a dirty smell in the air. Rain was now inevitable. The old man looked up at the sky, squinting as he did so.

"Not many people," I remarked.

"No. Most folk have enough sense to be indoors."

"Yes," I said. "I, er . . . I don't blame them."

"You'll wish you were one of them." He'd spoken the words so softly that I'd almost missed them.

"Sorry?"

"Nothin'," he replied, seeing my puzzled expression. "Just mental sewage. That'll be your boat there." He indicated the forlorn vessel on the sand. I looked at it, then looked back at him. He was staring up at the sky again, regarding it with what looked like contempt. As I felt the first few droplets of water land on my nose and cheeks, I wondered if the trip had been a good idea after all.

"So, does it have a motor?" It was all I could think of to say besides, *You don't seriously expect me to take that crate out onto the water, do you?*

"Yep," he replied, pulling his coat around him. "That'll be that big thing in the back." He removed a blue tarpaulin, revealing an outboard motor.

"Ah, right," I said.

"That'll be twenty quid. Cash."

"Oh . . . of course," I replied, fishing in my pockets for the money.

"And I'll want the boat back by nine tomorrow morning—in one piece."

I handed him the twenty-pound note, which he grabbed greedily. He turned and began walking back to his cabin, leaving me with the boat-shaped pile of driftwood. I would have mentioned to him that I hadn't been in a motorboat before, but he'd made it clear that our business, for now, was concluded. Once inside his office, he slammed the door. If I was going to get to the island before the heavens opened, I would have to move fast.

Thankfully, managing the boat was easier than I'd expected, and pretty soon I was cruising along the surface of Lake Languor. I had gone a considerable distance from the shore when there came a loud crack from above. The clouds were relieving themselves of their burden, and were not content to do so quietly. As far as I could tell, the boat was going as fast as it could, which wasn't fast enough. The cold rain pelted my face and hands, slowly numbing them. I looked to my left and saw in the distance what appeared to be my destination. I had been speeding toward the opposite end of the lake when I should have been going at an angle from the dock. I steered the boat to the left, correcting my course, and set the small land mass in my sights. There was another loud noise from the heavens and the shower became a deluge.

Before long, the rain was so heavy it was obscuring the view before me. The island was little more than a blurred shape. The surface of the lake was alive, water flying in all directions, and at times the boat lifted into the air before smacking down hard on the choppy surface. But right then soaking wet hair and clothes were the least of my worries. I didn't like the idea of the motor cutting out, leaving me stranded on the cold, deep expanse. It seemed unfair that the thick, gray clouds should gather above the lake and nowhere else. Nevertheless, I continued toward the island, the rain sheeting down and worsening, it seemed, by the second.

Pretty soon I was approaching the shore, so I cut the engine. Unfortunately, by the time I saw the sharp rock directly in the boat's path, it was too late. I was traveling too fast, even without the engine, and there was no way of avoiding a collision. I took hold of my bag and jumped over the side of the vessel into the cold, dark water.

Luckily, I hit nothing on my plunge into the lake, though there were rocks all around me. The water was far colder than I had expected, but thankfully, it only came up to my waist. My bag had been submerged briefly, so I held it up to stop it from being saturated further. I could do nothing but watch as the boat slammed against the rock and shattered into pieces. I hadn't expected the damage to be quite so bad. It was a good indication of the condition of the boat. I swore out loud, cursing the harbormaster for giving me such a wretched craft.

Holding up my bag, I waded onto the small beach and stood there dripping, swearing and gazing back out at the dark water. The pieces of wood that had once belonged to the boat were beginning to wash up on the sand. There wasn't a great deal that could be done about the wreck, and I started to panic at the thought of being stranded on the island. Still, Mather was sure to have his own boat, and would hopefully be sympathetic to my plight. I also remembered that my mobile phone was with me. It could well have been in contact with the water, but perhaps not for too long. I swung the bag over my shoulder, hoping that it could be dried out at the house, and walked up the slope, feeling tired, wet and sorry for myself. It was dark, it was raining and I seriously hoped the effort I'd made getting to the island wouldn't be wasted. Before long I saw a small light twinkling through the trees on the hill behind the beach.

At that moment my phone started to ring. It made an unusual garbled noise, and by the time I had fished it out of my bag it was silent, the screen blank. Either the battery was dead, or water had damaged the circuitry. Whatever the case, I was now cut off from civilization.

II: INITIATION

I trudged up the small incline where a rough path had been made between the trees and pushed my way through, water squelching in my shoes. I thought of all those pieces of boat washing against the rocks. I didn't know what I was going to say to the harbormaster when I got back to Tryst. Part of me wanted to avoid him altogether. It was a very dishonest thing to do, but I could be saving myself a lot of money. All he had was my name, so maybe he wouldn't bother trying to trace me.

Emerging from the undergrowth, I found myself facing a house. It wasn't quite what I had expected. I'm not sure why but I had imagined a quaint country cottage laden with ivy and roses. Instead, what I found was a low, gray-brick bungalow that appeared to have been constructed in a hurry. The roof was lower at one end, and the door, although it looked strong, seemed to have twisted slightly in its frame. Though its appearance was unique, there was simply no charm to the house at all. I wondered why anyone would choose to live in such an uncomfortable-looking place and in such seclusion, when at any moment they could be cut off from civilization entirely by a change in the weather.

I stepped into the porch, grateful to be out of the downpour. The doorway was just big enough to accommodate one person. I thought of Mather's letter and wondered, standing there on his doorstep, if I was about to meet another oddball, another eccentric loner who, after buckling under the stress of solitude, had reached out to someone—anyone—who might listen to him, even for a minute. I felt a moment of trepidation, but given how cold I was, I was willing to take a chance. Even if he turned out to be a raving lunatic, I would happily sit and listen to his jabbering, as long as I was warm and dry.

There was a strange trickling feeling near the ball of my right thumb, and I saw that it must have caught a rock on my drop into the water. The skin was red, and was already turning purple in places. Blood was seeping out of a small cut. As I put the wound to my mouth I felt sure I heard a gasp, and a woman uttering the words: *He's here!*

I stood still for a few seconds to listen, but could make out nothing more. Deciding it must have been a radio or television, I knocked on the door and waited. All I could hear now was the sound of water dripping from the edge of the porch, before the door finally opened.

Mather wasn't quite what I had expected either. From the tone of his letter I'd imagined a refined, educated man. Instead, I was greeted by a short, plump fellow with receding hair, old clothes and glasses that were thick-framed and slightly bent. You could tell from looking at him that he had little contact with the outside world. Either that, or there were no mirrors in the house. To me his overall appearance suggested a man of little intelligence; but his manner quickly dispelled that illusion.

"Mr. Reeves?" A tentative smile accompanied his inquiry.

"Yes. You must be Mr. Mather," I replied, droplets of water still falling from my hair.

"The very same!" His expression brightened. "Please—do come in." He ushered me inside the house, closing the door quickly against the rain. "I feel so guilty about you coming here in such awful weather. Did you have much trouble getting across the lake?"

"Well, yes. I, er . . . crashed the boat, I'm afraid. It's wrecked."

"No! My word. Are you all right?"

"Yes, I'm fine. Just a few bruises, but—"

"Good grief, how terrible, though." There was concern in his voice, as well as curiosity.

"I think I hit the rocks just offshore."

"You're lucky to be alive, then. And the water must have been freezing."

"Yes, it was a bit. But I'm fine, really," I assured him. "I should have checked the weather forecast before I left."

"Ah, yes. But even then one has to account for the unpredictability of nature."

"Mmm."

I followed him into the living room, conscious that water was dripping from my trousers. A fire had been lit, and without hesitation I dropped my bag and stood before the fireplace, absorbing the much-needed warmth. I handed Mather my coat, which he took elsewhere. He came back a short time later with a small wooden chair, which he placed next to me.

"Please sit and dry yourself. The bathroom is just down the hall if you need to use it. You might want to take a shower. I can dry your clothes for you in the meantime if you'd like."

I appreciated his generosity but didn't want to impose. "No, no, it's OK, really. It's just my trousers. I'm sure they'll dry out soon enough. I didn't bring a spare pair, unfortunately."

"Oh, I see, yes. I don't think a pair of mine would be of any use. You're nearly a foot taller than me," he said, holding his hands out in apology.

I smiled, a little nervously. However, I soon felt the heat surging through my clothes and body. "I think at this rate I'll be dry in no time," I said.

"Yes, I do hope so. Now then, how about some tea?" He glanced at the window as a flash of lightning illuminated the clearing outside.

"Anything hot would be great," I replied. "I'm anxious to hear about this mosquito of yours. It sounds fascinating." We could now hear the rain intensifying, accompanied by the occasional clap of thunder.

"Ah, all in good time. I have some cake or could make you a sandwich if you're hungry. You'll stay the night, of course? I couldn't possibly send you back out in this storm."

"Oh, er, I wouldn't want to impose. Besides, I've

arranged to stay at the Rocklyn Bluewater. Though now that I've lost my boat, I would appreciate it if you could help me get back to the mainland."

"Oh," he said, sounding rather disappointed. "Oh, I see. Well, of course, if you must stay there, then . . . And I would be glad to take you back to the mainland—it's just that the storm seems to be worsening and—"

"No, it's very kind of you, really, but I can expense it, so I may as well, you know . . ."

"Yes, of course—although once the lake is in the grip of a storm as violent as this one is turning out to be, sailing can be a difficult business. As you'll know from your unfortunate accident." The flames from the fire were dancing in the lenses of his spectacles. "Are you sure you're all right?"

"I'm fine, really." I smiled to try to reassure him. "I suppose . . . well, if it's going to be dangerous to go back out . . . I mean, I wouldn't want to put you to any—"

"Excellent! It's settled then. The spare room has already been arranged for this eventuality. Now then, are you sure I can't make you a sandwich?"

"Oh, yes, that would be great, thank you."

For a moment Mather seemed to detach himself from the conversation. Something cracked in the fire and woke him from his stupor.

"Oh, yes, of course, sandwich. Ha!" With that, he hurried out of the room again.

I cursed silently, annoyed by the predicament I now found myself in. A guest house was one thing; a stranger's house, especially one as secluded as this, was quite another.

I had a good look around the room. Aside from the erratic light generated by the fire, the only illumination was from a small oil lamp on a sideboard to my right. But despite the near gloom I could see a large number of books piled high on several shelves around me. And what at first looked like paintings or prints on the walls turned out, on closer scrutiny, to be silhouettes. I peered closely at one that was mounted above the fireplace. The artist had talent: the outline of a large butterfly with elaborate wings and long antennae had been expertly cut from black paper. It was perfect, and I found it hard to imagine the creature's actual shadow being any more impressive. I looked at a couple of other examples before Mather reappeared with a tray.

I returned to my chair and gulped down the tea, as Mather handed me a cheese and tomato sandwich on a plate. He sat down in an armchair, just behind me.

"The silhouettes," I began. "Did you do them yourself?" I turned to see his face brighten.

"I did indeed," he replied, glancing up at the butterfly picture above the mantelpiece. "Do you like them?"

"Mmm. They're very good."

"It's an honor I bestow on only the finest specimens nature has to offer. Rendering them in shadow, in black and white, takes away any pretense, any fancy. I love them for their shapes, you see, not their colors. It is the same principle with black-and-white photography. It exposes the truth, blanches out all the extravagance, revealing the true, naked image . . . the beauty." He sipped his tea. "An old friend of mine did the same thing with photographs of beautiful women. He insisted they were all ex-girlfriends." He laughed out loud. "If they were, then they must have been after him for something other than his looks. Still, what would I know about women?"

I suddenly remembered the female voice I'd heard while outside in the porch. "Do you live alone here, Mr. Mather?"

"Yes. Why do you ask?"

"Oh, it's just that I thought I heard a woman's voice when I was outside. Was it your television?"

"Heavens, no! I've never owned one of those infernal devices."

"Oh . . . a radio?"

Mather merely shook his head.

"I must have imagined it then."

"Don't worry, Mr. Reeves, we all hear voices from time to time. It's nothing to be concerned about."

"True." I looked back at the picture above the fire-place. "You certainly have a steady hand," I said.

"Yes. A steady hand and deep concentration come from my days as a surgeon. I'm retired now, but one never loses such skills."

"Where did you practice?" I took a bite of sandwich. It was good.

"Guy's Hospital for the first few years; then I moved

back to Charing Cross, where I originally studied. I retired early and moved here to follow my hobby."

"Etymology?"

"Ah." Mather smirked. "I think etymology is more your speciality than mine."

"Mmm?" I looked up from my sandwich, raising my eyebrows. Then I realized my mistake. "Oh, it's *entomology*, of course. I'm always getting those two mixed up."

"It's all right—I used to have the same problem, before my fascination with insects. Since then, nearly every book I've bought has had 'entomology' on the cover. I'd much rather leave the study of language and its complexities to others. I imagine it must seem like quite a fruitless pursuit sometimes, considering how every language is in a constant state of change."

"Yes. It's amazing how fast they can evolve."

"Ah, evolution," Mather said, staring into the fire. "Another interest of mine. So simple, yet at the same time so immeasurably complex. It's taken some pretty big leaps, but in the process has overlooked so much."

"Overlooked?" I put the last piece of sandwich into my mouth.

Mather seemed absorbed in the dancing light from the fire. "Well, for example," he said, almost in a daze, "haven't you ever wondered why, after all these millennia, our perspiration, while doing its job as well as ever, still smells and still stains our clothes?"

"I can't say I—"

"And blood—why is it bright red and not transparent like water? Why does it give us away so easily with its pungent aroma? It only makes a predator's job simpler."

"Maybe that's the point," I said. "Maybe it's nature's way of keeping a balance. I mean, if predators couldn't track their prey, they'd starve to death. They need some sort of advantage."

Mather chuckled to himself and chose not to pursue the subject, but what he said had puzzled me. I was beginning to wonder where all this was leading, and had determined to return to the purpose of my visit when Mather stood up suddenly and took the cups and plate back into the kitchen.

While the sound of jostling crockery and splashing water came from down the corridor, I went over to one of the shelves of hefty volumes. Large, dry patches had formed on my trousers. It looked as if I were wetting myself in reverse. As a result of the drying, an uncomfortable itchiness had broken out all over my body. I scratched my knee, then examined a couple of the titles on the shelf in front of me: *Manhunters of the Congo Basin* by M. Baxter, *The Queen of the Hive* by Hawke Ellison. One title in particular caught my eye: *Her Story* by R. H. Occum. The book lay on its side atop a row of similar editions. My curiosity aroused by the title, I picked it up.

The front cover featured a large pentagram with a mosquito in its center and unusual symbols dotted around it. Above it was the title, printed in an antique script, and below that the author's name in an equally elaborate font.

Leafing through the curious book, I saw that it wasn't only the cover that used such a unique typeface. The entire text was lovingly arranged and printed, the accompanying engravings also reproduced in great depth and detail. As I looked from one illustration to the other, I saw a pattern emerging. Each one featured a mosquito, quite large in size, attacking one or more screaming people. The first few pictures showed Roman centurions fleeing the beast as if for their lives. On the following pages were depictions of early Saxon Britons, medieval Europeans, then various cultures and countries up until very recent times. The same monster seemed to have been causing all sorts of problems throughout history. I scanned a few portions of the text. It was a collection of tales about a fabled creature known as the Devil's Hand—a formidable foe, judging by the damage it could cause. I prayed that the demon creature depicted in the book was in no way related to the Ganges Red. I had nearly finished leafing through the book when I became aware of a presence nearby.

"Quite a collection," I said nervously, turning to see Mather standing behind me in the doorway.

"Thank you," he replied. "*Many a quaint and curious volume of forgotten lore,* as the poem goes." He walked over and looked at the book in my hands. "I was quite an avid collector once upon a time. I used to spend hours scouring secondhand bookstores. It was an absolute joy to find that one." I handed him the book. He ran his hands over the cover. "Have you heard of the legend of Nhan Diep?"

"No, I don't think so."

"Ah, it's a marvelous story in here from old Vietnam."

"Oh? My grandmother was Vietnamese."

"Really?"

"Yes. She met my grandfather when he went over to fight in the war in 'sixty-six. He was an American pilot."

"Oh. Well, perhaps she knows the story. It's quite a popular—"

"I'm afraid she passed away a few years ago."

"Oh, I'm very sorry." There was an uncomfortable pause.

"So . . . would it be possible to see the Ganges Red? I'm anxious to get a good look at it. I wish I'd done a little more research before coming. I don't know anything about it, I have to confess."

"Ah," Mather said, softly clapping his hands together. "I'm afraid it isn't a good idea to disturb her at this hour. I fed her not long ago and she's always a little irritable after feeding time. Best if we tackle that tomorrow."

"What is it about the mosquito that led you to contact me?"

"Oh, so many things. The Ganges Red is the only example of her kind."

"Really?"

"Oh, yes. And her size will quite stun you. She is too large even to be considered a freak of nature. No . . ." Mather gazed up in what almost looked like reverence. "She is something else entirely. Many cultures have worshipped the Ganges Red. Accounts of this can be found in *Her Story*."

"Oh, right. As well as the legend of, er . . ."

"Nhan Diep," he said, pronouncing the words slowly to make sure I got them this time.

"Right, yes."

"You can borrow the book for tonight if you like. A little reading always helps me sleep. And it will set your imagination alight in anticipation of tomorrow's introduction," he said, nodding his assurance.

"Yes, I'd be happy to take a look. I don't reckon I'll have too much trouble falling asleep tonight, though."

"Quite." He handed me the book.

I decided it wouldn't hurt to have a scan through it in case it could be used in the article. I couldn't think of anything more to say. My unease must have been noticeable, as Mather said, "I do apologize for any inconvenience, Mr. Reeves, and will try to provide every accommodation to ensure you feel comfortable and welcome, which, of course . . . you are. Very much so."

"Oh, thank you. I'm . . . It's fine, really."

"Well, I like to retire to bed early, so I'll see you in the morning. I promise to make up for tonight by giving you the story of a lifetime tomorrow. No doubt you have had dealings with many charlatans, Mr. Reeves. But you'll be very glad in the morning, when you discover that I am quite different. The bathroom is at your disposal should you like to take a bath or shower. Why don't I show you to your room, then you can use the facilities."

"Oh, yes. Of course." I followed, tucking *Her Story* under my arm and picking up my damp bag on the way

41

out. Mather's hospitality was welcome after my troubled journey across the lake, but I was still left with an uneasy feeling that I couldn't seem to shake off. Nevertheless, I didn't want to upset him. So far there seemed no real reason for me to be concerned.

"I'll light the fire in there. If your bag's still wet, it should dry quickly by the fireplace."

"Thanks, that's great."

Mather led me to the modest bathroom. The suite might once have been champagne in color, possibly even beige—it was hard to tell: time had washed much of the color out. It was clean, however, as was the rest of the room. Mather appeared to be a particularly neat individual.

The guest bedroom was small but cozy and looked as if it had been cleaned recently. The bed was freshly made, the covers turned back. I dropped my bag by the side of it as Mather busied himself with lighting the fire. In minutes it was roaring.

I dropped the book he had given me on the bed and stood by the small bedroom window, looking out into the dark. The wind and rain continued to torment the trees, but the thunder and lightning had passed.

"Did anyone live here before you?" I asked, as Mather stood, adjusting his spectacles.

"Ah," he said, joining me by the window. "The previous owner was the one who built the house. He lived here for quite a while, but in the end, being elderly, he went to live with his daughter. I saw the house advertised in a newspaper. It looked like such a wonderful place.

True, it was a big step into the unknown coming to live here, but the rewards . . . I've been reaping ever since." He smiled.

"So, how long have you been here?"

"Oh, nearly five years, I think. Yes . . ." He seemed lost for a second or two, as though some memory had caught him by surprise. "Excuse me, will you? The dishes require my attention." He sniffed and walked off in the direction of the kitchen.

I sat down on the bed and stared at my bag, from which wisps of steam were rising. A short time later I was sure I could hear Mather talking. He had been alone for so long, I could imagine that talking to himself was a habit he had fallen into very easily.

My host soon returned; he walked over to the fire, picked up my bag and felt the outside of it.

"Hmm. I think you may need to empty this and check everything individually. Water can get everywhere." He looked at me, took off his glasses and proceeded to rub them on his jumper. "You do look a little washed out, if you'll excuse the pun. I hope you haven't caught a cold."

I did feel pretty exhausted. The small-scale shipwreck and unpleasant weather had come as a shock to the system. I needed to rest.

"Well, I tell you what," Mather said. "I'll leave you to use the bathroom and get settled in. Why don't you join me for breakfast at about eight o'clock tomorrow—then we can get started on the story."

"That sounds good," I enthused. "I can't wait to see this mosquito of yours."

"Ah . . ." Mather smiled. "All in good time. I'll be reading in my room for a while if you need me. Don't be afraid to knock." He turned to leave.

"Right. Thank you very much." It was only then that the whole absurdity of the situation struck me. There I was, sleeping in a strange room in a strange house with a fairly strange man, to meet some strange (if genuine) creature. There was also the fact that I'd nearly drowned. I had a sudden, bizarre feeling that I was in someone else's dream. Right then sleep was a very good idea. I made a decision to use the bathroom, then go straight to bed.

Thunder clapped again outside the window. The storm hadn't yet finished with the island. I looked at my watch. Water had found its way beneath the glass, enlarging and warping the numbers. It was a few minutes past nine o'clock. I grabbed the wash bag that had been drying by the fire and left the room.

I could hear the rainfall resuming with vigor as I walked along to the bathroom. There was a strong smell of disinfectant or bleach that I hadn't noticed before. The shower curtain that ran around the circumference of the bath on a flimsy rail looked fairly new, almost unused. I washed, relishing the feeling of warm water on my face.

Minutes later, back in the bedroom and undressed, I pondered a little more on my situation. Aside from Mather's boat, I knew of no other way off the island. I looked at my bag, now placed at a safe distance from the fire. Picking it up, I fished out my mobile phone and pushed the power button. Nothing happened.

Unclipping the battery cover, I groaned as water dripped onto my knee. I put the phone on the floor near the grate, where it could dry out slowly. For the time being there was no way of contacting anyone. Not that I thought I would need to call for help at that point. I just felt slightly vulnerable without that vital link to civilization. The tape recorder, thankfully, was dry, as was the camera. Its carry case was a little damp, but on opening it I was overjoyed to see that little or no water had found its way inside.

I placed the camera on the floor by the bed and turned to look at the dancing flames. It was rare that I had the opportunity to appreciate an open fire, but I had a feeling that the desire to fall asleep would soon overtake me.

Before giving in to my exhaustion altogether, I slipped between the soft clean sheets and started reading *Her Story*.

Far back in the mystery-shrouded past of old Vietnam, there was once a young, hardworking farmer named Ngoc Tam. He was an honest, generous man, who had taken for his wife a beautiful girl from a neighboring village. Nhan Diep was a slender girl, full of life and good humor, but being a restless spirit she soon grew tired and disillusioned with farming, and longed for a life of luxury.

One day, without warning, she fell horribly ill and

slipped into a weak, debilitating torpor. Tam found her lying on the ground and carried her back to the house. But despite his best efforts to revive her, Diep died in her distraught husband's arms. Tam was inconsolable and wept for days. He shunned the help of friends and family and refused to leave the body of his wife or allow her to be buried.

Tam didn't know how he could live without his precious Diep. In desperation he sold all his assets and bought a raft and a beautiful casket in which he placed the body of his wife. Taking the raft to the nearby stream, he set sail with an innate hope that somehow he could find a cure for his broken heart. On the twenty-second day of his journey, help found him.

He woke from a troubled sleep that morning to find that the raft had stopped at the foot of a mountain. Leaving the raft and the casket behind, he soon found himself climbing across a carpet of a thousand rare flowers. He stopped in a small clearing, then, as he continued up the mountain, he noticed an old man on the path before him, leaning on a curious bamboo staff. The man had long white hair that floated gently on the caressing breeze and wrinkled, sunburned skin. Tam felt as though somehow this stranger already knew him.

At once it dawned on Tam that the old man was in fact Tien Thai, the genie of medicine. Tam fell to his knees, his hands clasped together, and pleaded with the genie to restore his beloved to life.

"Ngoc Tam, I know of you and your virtues," the old man said. "But your wife's hold on you is still strong.

It will not be relinquished. You must learn to grow, not suffer from your love for her."

"But I cannot live any kind of life without her. I beg you, if it is within your power, bring my Diep back to life."

The genie replied, "I shall not deny your request, for your love and grief are sincere, but I have seen great men entrust their hearts to the whims of selfish, fickle women. I have watched women of wonderful wisdom surrender themselves whole to the mercy of evil, heartless men. In a way I am glad that I do not understand— to do so must be terrible."

Ngoc Tam was at once defiant. "You have no idea how wonderful a creature my wife is. I have loved nothing in life like I have loved her. I must have her back, or life itself is pointless."

The old genie sighed. "Very well, then," he conceded. "Do this: pierce your finger with a thorn from one of the bushes over there and let three drops fall on the body of your wife. Do this and she shall return to you."

Tam jumped to his feet, rushed over to a large bush and snapped off a nasty-looking thorn. He thanked the genie profusely as he ran back down the path.

Tam nearly fell into the water in his desperation to get onto the raft. He scrambled on, lifted the lid from the casket and pricked his left forefinger with the thorn. Three drops of his blood fell onto Nhan Diep's exposed palm.

Diep opened her eyes as though awakening from a deep sleep. Her wrinkled, pale skin suddenly bloomed with color and vitality. She gasped and sat up, looking around. Tam took her in his arms and hugged her passionately.

The genie had followed Tam, and now approached the couple slowly. His eyes met Diep's. "Forget not your obligations, Nhan Diep," the genie said to her. "Remember your husband's devotion to you. Return his love, and work hard." He turned from the emotional couple, saying only, "Go now. May you both be happy."

The story was compelling and I was tempted to read on, curious to find out what it had to do with the mosquito, but my eyelids were like lead weights, and I no longer had the strength to keep them open. I put down the book on the bedside table, wondering if my grandmother had ever told me the story when I was younger. Some of my earliest memories are of her reading to me late at night, her enthusiasm for the folktales of her native people and her talent for voices never failing to delight me. *"One more, Nanna! One more!"* I'd insist, and she would nearly always give me another story, and another, until I fell asleep, feeling happy and loved.

With the bedside lamp off, the room fell into darkness. As my eyes slowly adjusted, I was able to make out the various shapes of the furniture. I felt a little homesick and longed for the comfort and familiarity of my own room. In the shadows the single bookcase opposite the bed was a black, angular monolith. Looking up at the ceiling, I remembered how imprecise the house's dimensions had appeared from outside. There was a triangular gap between the top of the bookcase and the ceiling, which meant that one or the other wasn't level. Staring at it for a few seconds, I began to feel queasy, so I shifted onto my left side and looked toward the window.

As I closed my eyes, I reflected that Mather had appeared to be a pretty friendly individual. But there was an element of mystery about him, as if he was holding something back. I had a feeling that his story, whether genuine or not, was certainly worth pursuing, if only to learn more about him. My thoughts remained centered on my host, the house and the promise Mather's letter had held, until at some point my mind swam and sleep claimed me.

The next time my eyes opened there were tears in them. I was no longer in bed, but standing on a raft, floating down a wide stream with only a large casket for company. Suddenly the raft stopped at the foot of a huge, flower-carpeted mountain, from which drifted the most enchanting of scents. As though my body had a mind of its own, I stepped onto the land and soon found myself walking beneath colorful, fruit-laden trees. My ascent continued, until I stopped in a small clearing to catch my breath. It was then that I noticed the old man on the path before me, leaning on a curious bamboo staff. His hair was long and white and floated gently on the breeze; his skin was dark, leathery and wrinkled, but his large eyes were youthful, with a playful spark. A white cape of thin, almost transparent material billowed out behind and around him, while his body was wrapped in a bright blue robe that sparkled in the sun.

He introduced himself as Tien Thai, the genie of medicine, and seemed to know who I was.

"Ngoc Tam, I know of you and your virtues," the old man said. "You are a good and loving man."

I told him all I cared about was my beloved.

"Your wife's hold on you is still strong, Ngoc Tam," he continued, "but you must allow the wound of your loss to heal. Accept that love is now denied you, then truly you can live."

"No," I insisted. "I won't leave her like this. I cannot go on without the love of my life. I may as well be dead too!"

"You must accept—"

"No," I screamed in defiance. "I cannot!" My hands were clenched into fists. A fierce torment was shaking my body, contracting my muscles into knots.

The old man looked long and hard at me, then seemed to adopt an expression of disappointed resignation. "Very well, then," he conceded. "If that is your choice. Do this: pierce your finger with a thorn from one of the bushes over there and let three drops fall on the body of your departed wife. Do this and she shall return to you."

I walked over to a large mass of rosebushes. I snapped off a particularly vicious-looking thorn, then ran off back down the path.

Leaping onto the raft, I lifted the lid from the casket

and saw the pitiful, deflated body of what could once have been a beautiful woman. I pricked my left forefinger with the thorn and squeezed out three drops of blood, so that they fell on her exposed palm.

As she opened her eyes, I awoke.

III: EXPLORATION

For quite some time I lay in bed, just thinking about the dream. It had been so real, so unlike any I'd had before. Every dream is wild and unique in its own way, but the one I had that night was something else.

Before long I grew bored with watching the daylight claim the room. I got out of bed, had a quick wash and dressed. Finding the house quiet and Mather still in his room, I decided to get some fresh air and clear my head of the powerful and bizarre images left over from the dream. Although I was eager to record Mather's story, he had said breakfast would be at eight o'clock, and I didn't want to appear rude or ungrateful by disturbing him too early. My watch told me it was only ten minutes past seven.

I took pains to be quiet as I drew the large bolt across the top of the front door. Opening it, I was confronted by a great blanket of mist that lay close to the ground outside and gave the small clearing a strange, ethereal quality.

I walked some way from the house, wading through the mist. I was amazed at how thick it actually was. It swirled and parted as I made my way through the trees before emerging by the shore. The mist was thinner on the water, yet it hugged the surface for as far as I could see. I gazed across the lake and tried to spy the town and the dock, but the mist obscured them. I couldn't see anything besides rocks, trees and water.

Gazing up at the sky, I fell into a kind of daze, hypnotized by the passing of the clouds. With some effort I wrenched my attention away and looked for traces of the boat I'd destroyed the day before. There was nothing, not even one piece of wood bobbing through the fog or washed up on the shore. I wondered where Mather's boat might be. I guessed it was sheltered somewhere, perhaps in a boathouse, where it would be safe from storms and unable to drift away. As there was still plenty of time before breakfast, I decided to take a further look around.

I returned to the house, then walked past it to the left, where I found a rough footpath heading into the trees. I could feel the air getting warmer and saw that the mist around my ankles was already thinning. I had a good feeling that the day would turn out to be brighter and calmer than the one before, and I wished my journey from London had been delayed by a day. At least then I might have had a boat to give back to the harbormaster.

Although the footpath was generally unobstructed, I still had to push my way through branches and bushes in order to make progress. There was a wonderful floral smell, and the silence that pervaded the whole area was soothing.

The path zigzagged through the trees until it opened out into another, smaller clearing. To the left was a large pile of rocks, beyond which was a wide-open view of the lake. I walked over and saw that a rough dirt slope ran down to a small sandy beach. Almost hidden among over-hanging branches from the trees above was a shed. It was green, but the paint had faded and flaked from years in the sun. I approached it for a closer inspection.

The shed had been constructed, rather hastily by the look of it, from vertical planks of wood. The door was padlocked, but through a thin gap between two of the planks I was able to get a glimpse of the interior. Shafts of light penetrated inside, revealing a large blue plastic sheet covering what I assumed was a boat. On impulse, I tried pulling the padlock apart, but it wouldn't budge. The lock, unlike the shed, was designed to withstand the rigors of nature.

As I turned from the shed and began to stroll along the small beach, I heard a sound like a door slamming somewhere far off. Mather must have become aware of my absence and was now out looking for me.

I headed back to the house, thinking as I did so that living on the island might not be so bad after all. In sum-mer the lake must be beautiful. I walked briskly, enjoy-ing the feel of the early morning sun on my face. Once back in the clearing, I caught a glimpse of Mather as he disappeared through the trees toward the other beach. I followed, and found him in a state of bewilderment, pac-ing up and down the sand, squinting and scanning the horizon. I stood for a while and watched as he went a few paces into the water, soaking his shoes and socks.

"Mr. Mather," I called, feeling it was time to put an end to his agitation.

He turned, and though he was startled by the sound of my voice, his relief was immediate. A smile lit up his face and he advanced toward me, apparently unaware of the water he was splashing onto his trousers. "Thank goodness," he said, his eyes wide open, making his expression all the more odd. "For a minute I was . . . I thought I'd lost you."

"No, no. I woke up early and couldn't get back to sleep so I decided to go for a walk."

Mather paused a moment, as though examining my face for evidence of something. "I'm sorry there's so little to see here." He looked down at his legs, noticing for the first time that his ankles were underwater. "Oh dear, oh dear. Look at me." He hopped about comically until he was back on the sand.

"I really am sorry to have worried you," I said.

"That's no problem. How . . . how far did you get?"

We started walking back up the bank to the trees, Mather shaking his drenched trousers in vain.

"Just to the beach on the other side of the island. The one with the shed."

"Ah, the boathouse." There was a nervousness in his voice that confused me. I hadn't been trying to leave the island. It may simply have been my safety he'd been concerned about, but he'd still seemed a little overanxious about my whereabouts. "I keep it locked," he said, matter-of-factly.

"You're not worried about the boat being stolen, though, are you? I had the impression that you didn't have many visitors."

"No, I don't. It's just that"—he smiled a little in embarrassment—"I have a tendency to be rather obsessive about security. I know it's silly, being so isolated, but, well, I can't help it. If the boat did disappear, then I'd—"

"Don't worry, I understand. And you've no need to worry about me taking off with it."

"No, of course not. I wasn't implying that—I suppose I get anxious too easily." He laughed. "Please ignore me—think no more of it."

Mather opened the front door and we went back into the house.

"Why don't you take a seat in the living room while I make us some breakfast?" he said, trailing his words behind him as he left the room.

"OK," I replied, hoping we would get to the matter at hand soon. "Thank you. I hope it will be all right to get started on the story in a little while. I really should be getting back to work as soon as possible."

"I perfectly understand," came the reply from the kitchen. "And I do apologize for detaining you. Blasted weather! I assure you it will be a story worth waiting for, though. The Lady will quite take your breath away." I presumed by "the Lady" he meant the mosquito, but it seemed an odd choice of words.

"Excellent," I replied, though Mather may have been out of earshot. I felt a little uneasy being left there on my own, not really knowing what to do with myself. Unable to sit still, I left the living room and crossed the hall to the kitchen.

This was also at the front of the house, its window looking out onto the clearing. It wasn't as big as I had expected, but since Mather lived on his own, I guessed it was more than adequate. There was, as I had expected, a gas stove, but there were also a number of electrical appliances—a refrigerator, kettle and toaster. Mather stood with his back to me, absorbed in thought.

"So, where's the generator?" I asked, startling him for the second time that morning.

He scratched his forehead and nodded toward the back of the building. "The previous owner had it installed inside a soundproofed hut behind the house. It's a fairly small gas-powered model. Thankfully, I don't need to go in there and replace the fuel very often. I use little electricity, really, but God forbid it should ever break down."

"Yes, that must be quite a scary thought. So, are there any other buildings on the island?" I asked as he filled the kettle with water. He set it on its plastic cradle and pressed the switch, then turned to me with a look that implied he didn't welcome my curiosity.

"Sorry if I'm being nosy," I said. "It comes with the job, I'm afraid."

Mather chuckled at this. "Not at all. I should have been prepared for it." He opened the breadbox and took out a sliced loaf. "No, this is the only building on the island." I wondered how often he went to the mainland for food. He must have made frequent trips, if he used bread and fresh foods rather than canned. Either that, or he arranged to have his groceries delivered. He took out four thin slices of bread and put them into the toaster.

"You'll love the Lady. I really can't wait for you to see her."

"Yes, I'm looking forward to it." I wasn't quite sure if I meant this or not. I still didn't know if Mather was telling the truth, or whether his story about this mosquito being the only one of its kind was a pack of lies. He turned from the toaster and took some plates out of the cupboard above the sink.

"So, Mr. Reeves . . . how are you with mosquitoes?"

"Sorry?"

"What do you know about them?"

"Oh, not a great deal, really. Only that they never leave me alone when I'm on vacation. I pulled a huge one off my leg last year in Jamaica. Stamped on it. I don't like killing things, but then he'd only have tried to get me again, wouldn't he?"

"She," Mather said.

"Pardon?"

"She." He left the word in the air while I stood in the doorway feeling slightly puzzled. He dropped a couple of tea bags into a faded brown teapot and said, "*She* would have tried again, not *he*. Only the female mosquito bites people."

"Oh, I see." I watched Mather take the kettle and pour

the boiling water into the pot. "So the males don't bother people?"

"Well," Mather began, putting the kettle back in its cradle. His expression was serious, but I sensed he was enjoying the informal tutorial. "There are cases of males biting people, but it's a very rare occurrence. They're probably just . . . confused."

"Confused? You mean, they thought they were girls?"

Mather gave me an odd look, clearly unappreciative of my stab at humor. "Well, not quite. They just made a mistake, that's all. It happens." He sounded a little frustrated with the direction the conversation was taking. "Males feed on vegetation, you see. Females do the same, but they need to ingest blood because the protein it contains facilitates egg production."

"I see. So it's more for breeding purposes than for sustenance?"

"That's right. The blood meal is purely to aid reproduction."

"So I squished a lady. How rude of me."

"Indeed." Mather placed cups and plates on a large tray. "Would you mind giving me a hand?"

"Of course not."

He added a large plate of toast, some butter and jam, and a couple of napkins. "I'll bring the rest in," he said.

"Right." I turned and left the kitchen, taking the tray into the living room, where I set it down on the small table by an armchair. Mather followed shortly with the tea. It was only then that I realized how hungry I was. Sitting down in one of the armchairs, I set about filling my stomach.

The birds were still singing in the trees outside as I ate the toast, pausing only to wash it down with gulps of tea. Once more I was struck with the feeling that I might have had a wasted journey. I was keen to conclude my business on the island and get started on the journey back to London. I did, after all, have a job to get back to. Nevertheless, I decided to delay a while longer before saying something that might sound rude. Sitting back in the chair with my tea, I waited for him to resume the conversation. He had the detached look that had been so common among my lecturers at university. I guess he too believed that a speech should be thought through as much as possible in advance, instead of being delivered unprepared. Only when he had finished his first piece of toast did he continue.

"You see, Mr. Reeves, the male mosquito is of no real interest to entomologists," he began, cleaning his teeth with his tongue. "He is little more than a drone. Once fertilization has taken place, he's out of the picture. He can do what he likes until he finally expires. It is the female that really matters."

"I see."

"*She* is the one who penetrates us—violates us, if you like." He grinned.

"Right. So tell me a little about malaria," I said, trying to get to the point of my visit.

"Malaria?" He took a sip of tea, eyeing me curiously.

"Yes. How does a mosquito pass it on? Where does it get it from in the first place?"

Mather looked through the window into the distance to my left. He broke a piece of toast off his second slice and put it in his mouth. He was clearly relishing a perhaps rare opportunity to educate another on his favorite subject.

"A lot of people wrongly assume," he said, still chewing, "that the mosquito somehow introduced malaria to the world and proceeded to spread it from human to human like some flying poisoned needle."

A plane passed overhead, temporarily breaking my host's narrative. Perhaps the isolation of the island had already got to me, as the sound of the plane seemed like a reassuring connection to the outside world. Mather waited until the sound had gone altogether.

"You see, the mosquito is a disease vector. It doesn't create the disease, it only carries it. After ingesting the blood of an infected person, it will fly off and unknowingly incubate the malaria parasite until it feeds on another human, passing it into their bloodstream, where it multiplies and attacks. Malaria isn't something mosquitoes are born with, you see; they have to feed on someone infected with it. It's the same with yellow fever, dengue and the West Nile virus. The mosquito is extremely proficient at disease transmission, even though it's completely unaware of what's going on."

"We're lucky to still be here, then," I said.

"Hmm." Mather considered this briefly. "Well, possibly. You have to bear in mind that there are a lot of factors that affect a certain species or a certain disease. If there were, say, a thousand times more mosquitoes in the world than there are now, they might spend too much of their time attacking each other over territory to be bothered with us. If they didn't destroy themselves, they might end up wiping out the diseases they carry by spreading them too thin. Perhaps the more a disease is spread, the less potent it is, and the more resistant we become. But"— he chuckled—"it's all guesswork, I'm afraid. I'm no expert on tropical diseases, I'm just theorizing. Although, everything in nature is exhaustible. Nothing is infinite if you look far enough down the timeline. If a certain disease became more widespread, there's a chance that the human race could become more resistant to it, and the symptoms, in time, could be less severe. But we're not talking about the common cold. Malaria is pretty hostile and it's unlikely we'll ever become resistant to it." He stopped, pondering what he'd said. "It's a most interesting subject, though. I'm sure someone's written a book about it."

Although it was nowhere near as interesting as the story I'd come to the island for, there was a chance I could use some of what Mather had said as the basis for an article, bolstered perhaps by information I might find on the Internet. Derek had told me to return with something. Perhaps a story about mosquitoes and mosquito theories would be a good enough substitute. Something rational and thought-provoking might even make a nice change for the magazine.

"Excuse me a moment," Mather said, setting his cup down on the tray and rising to his feet. "I won't be a second. Have you finished?" He gestured toward my tea.

I drained the last of it, then gave him the cup. "Thanks. I'm not a big tea drinker, but that was very good."

"You're welcome." He picked up the tray and left the room. I heard him put it down in the kitchen and run some water. A few minutes later I heard the sound of footsteps in the corridor and what I guessed was the bathroom door closing.

While Mather was away, I took another look around the living room. Now that more daylight had been allowed in, it seemed bigger. I went over to the piles of books, crammed together on the shelves opposite the window. Some of them were very old; many were bound in a thick material, embossed in some cases with lettering and patterns. Some volumes seemed to be falling apart: loose pages were poking out from them. I picked up one of these editions for a closer look, careful not to cause any further damage, and realized that it wasn't falling apart at all. The pages that stuck out in various places were actually from other books. Mather seemed to be using them as bookmarks. Why he would want to do such a thing was a mystery, unless the pages had been torn from a book he would otherwise have thrown away. Given the number of books he had, though, it was hard to believe that Mather could be so destructive.

The book in my hands was an anatomical textbook called *Body Ratio* by the Reverend C. N. Tantica. There were countless pages from another book, which must have been somewhat smaller, judging by the difference in page size, inserted at regular intervals. I opened the book to one of the marked pages and found a drawing that depicted a human liver. Checking a few of the other bookmarked pages, I found further diagrams of various organs. Mather had clearly studied the book in detail at some point, probably during his days as a medical student. It seemed to be well looked after, being practically dust-free, unlike many of the other titles.

Turning from the bookcase, I noticed another of Mather's framed silhouettes hanging to the left of the window. I don't know why I hadn't spotted it before, because it was striking. It must have been concealed in shadow the previous night, but now, in daylight, was hard to miss. Judging by the long feeding tube that extended from its head, it was a mosquito and was about the size of a small bird. Written beneath the finely crafted image in clear, elegant handwriting were the words:

Ganges Red
(Actual Size)

"Big, isn't she?" Mather said from the doorway.

I jumped in surprise. "Yes, it certainly is." I found it hard to tear my attention away from the picture. "It's not actually that big, though, is it?"

"Oh, yes, indeed. And if you'll follow me, I'll prove it." He turned and walked off down the corridor. With some trepidation, but also a hope that I might finally get to see something of interest, I followed.

Mather's bedroom was larger than I had expected, with wooden panels extending from ceiling to floor, all beautifully sanded and stained. Even the floor was bare wood and colored to match the walls. Arranged neatly around the panels were more of the delicate and elaborate insect silhouettes. There were two more mosquitoes, another butterfly, a hornet, what looked like a praying mantis and something else that I didn't recognize. To the right of his small bed, under the room's only window, was a handsome rolltop desk. In general, Mather's room was tidy, almost minimalist in arrangement.

He walked over to the right wall and took hold of a long, thin horizontal panel that split the wood in two. The whole right side of the panel slid across, revealing a large compartment behind the wall. The space was occupied by a single glass tank. The lid was metal, perhaps brass, and etched with delicate, swirling patterns, as were the strips that ran down each corner—fitted, perhaps, for extra strength. The glass panels had yellowed, so I guessed the tank had been in use for some time. I realized then that up until that point I'd assumed the insect to be dead. It seemed, however, that this was not the case, and the fact that Mather kept the creature in his bedroom left me a little bothered.

"Fear not," Mather said, gently tapping the front of

the glass box. "She sleeps during the day, so it's some-times necessary to give her some encouragement." He waited for a couple of seconds, but nothing happened.

I studied the leaves, grass and twigs that filled almost a third of the container, hoping to spot some movement. Remaining unruffled by the no-show of his exhibit, Mather drummed his fingers lightly on the glass, then stepped back, a look of satisfaction on his face. I then heard a whining sound coming from within the glass prison. I was still prepared for disappointment. However, to my combined surprise and horror, a mosquito far bigger than it had any right to be detached itself from the underside of the lid where it had been hiding, and dropped, turn-ing itself over in midair to hover before our faces.

IV: PRESENTATION

A remarkable thing occurred during my introduction to the Ganges Red. I was assaulted by a brief yet piercing headache unlike any I'd experienced before. It was as though, for a moment, an inaudible scream echoed through my mind, straining to be heard but achieving only pain. I rubbed my temples as it subsided, and concentrated on the tank. The Ganges Red was simply awesome, and if I hadn't gazed upon it with my own eyes, I'd have had a hard time believing the size of the creature.

It stopped hovering and attached itself to the glass panel, perhaps to get a better look at us. The oversized body of the insect was a deep, glistening red, a color that seemed to indicate danger. On her abdomen were several wide, broken black stripes. Even her long, needle-like feeding tube was red, making me wonder what a sight she must be after feeding.

"Quite the study in scarlet, isn't she?" Arms folded, Mather stood watching me, relishing my reaction. I might have been shocked, perhaps even scared to begin with, but I couldn't help but admire the unique beauty of the creature.

"She's incredible. I didn't think it was possible for a

mosquito to be so big." She could have wrapped herself around a tennis ball and been able to cross her legs. Her wingspan alone must have been over twenty centimeters. I turned my attention to the lid of the tank, feeling a momentary sense of panic.

"I don't think I will ever tire of looking at her," Mather said, clearly enraptured.

There came a scratching at the window. I turned to see a rather dirty and disheveled-looking cat. Its fur was damp and matted in a number of places and half its right ear was missing. I was about to mention the visitor to Mather when he spoke.

"That," he said, clearly unimpressed at the sight of the animal, "is Mr. Hopkins. The rather scruffy bane of my existence."

"He's not yours, then?"

"Certainly not," Mather replied, as if insulted. "I would never associate with such an unpleasant animal." He walked over to the window. For a minute I thought he might shout or bang on the pane, but he just stood there glaring at the poor creature. "He must have sneaked onto the island by stowing away on my boat."

Mr. Hopkins remained on the window ledge, his forlorn expression matching his physical appearance. He seemed about as impressed with Mather as Mather was with him.

"Why do you call him Mr. Hopkins?"

Mather turned his attention away from the mangy feline, and replied, "Because he reminds me of a neighbor

I had many years ago. Awful man. Couldn't keep his nose out of my business. *He* was a scruffy ratbag too."

I thought the animal possessed a certain charm, but being a cat lover, I was biased. Mr. Hopkins pawed at the glass again and seemed to look directly at me.

"Blasted animal," my host erupted, perhaps concerned that the cat was trying to steal the show. He knocked three times on the pane. The cat merely blinked and continued eyeing me.

I winced as another sharp pain shot through my head. Looking back at the mosquito, I noticed that its head was tilted in the direction of the window. A strange thought occurred to me, something that I now find very hard to put into words. I knew that the bizarre situation might have been affecting my judgment, but even that didn't feel like a sufficient explanation for what I was feeling. It was as though I had stumbled into the middle of a conversation that I was unable to comprehend.

To clear my head a little I excused myself and returned to my room to retrieve my tape recorder. I actually felt a little more positive about my trip. The insect was remarkable. I couldn't wait to get some photographs of it, and could imagine it gracing the magazine's front cover. Returning to Mather's room, I sat at his desk to begin the interview.

"Do you mind?" I asked, indicating the recording device.

"Oh no, not at all," he replied, lingering by the window, where he could keep an eye on the cat.

"So, where did you find her?"

"Mmm? Oh, I have a number of acquaintances— fellow collectors, you might say—in various countries. An old friend of mine in Zaire wrote to me some years ago with the news that sightings of the Ganges Red were on the increase. Stories about her had been circulating near his research post for decades, and, being busy on numerous projects, he couldn't find the time to look into all of them. He was skeptical about the existence of a creature that had eluded capture for so long. I have to admit, I'd had doubts for many years myself. Nevertheless, I pressed him to at least talk to some of the native people who claimed to have seen her. He relented and for the next few weeks, when he had the time to spare, he made enquiries, interviewed certain individuals. He wrote back some time later, detailing a number of testimonies that all pointed to the same conclusion. The Ganges Red, or something fitting her description, was alive and well."

"But she isn't the only one, is she? I mean, surely if these sightings are real, they are of different insects?"

"I wasn't sure at first, but to my surprise I found myself beginning to believe the mythology surrounding her. And there have been no more sightings since she came into my possession."

Mather paused for a while, during which all I could hear was the grinding noise made by the tape recorder. He turned his back to the window and leaned against the sill.

"I yearned to travel to Africa myself, but I had grown

too accustomed to my life here. I always feel anxious whenever I think about leaving. Instead, I made a plea to my friend to find the Lady himself, whatever it took. I told him that I would cover any necessary expenses. As it turned out, he had begun to share my excitement and had already started making arrangements. A week later an assistant of his came across a small cave near a river." He nodded toward the tank. "She was inside, along with thousands of smaller mosquitoes, most likely from the *Aedes aegypti* family. Unfortunately, the assistant and his guides died in their attempt to capture her. My friend found their bodies when he arrived at the cave some days later. Thanks to his experience in capturing dangerous insects, he was able to secure her almost without incident."

"Almost?" I asked.

"Well, it sounds incredible, but my friend claimed the Lady possessed an ability to . . . communicate." Mather rubbed his head. "I know how it sounds, but many occurrences in nature are difficult to comprehend."

"Yes, that's true," I replied, more to keep him talking than anything else. Not for a moment was I prepared to believe that an insect could talk.

"Mother Nature loves a paradox, as an old friend used to say to me," Mather continued. "And how right he was. Our Lady here is a living testament to that." He left the window and went back over to the recess, placing his hand on the glass and concealing the insect. "Scientifically, she shouldn't exist—has no right to exist. And yet here she is, in all her astounding glory. I gave her a name of my own, you know. I felt rather odd doing it as she is hardly a pet, but I felt a compulsion of sorts. I initially thought of calling her Isis; then some short time later I had a vivid dream about her. I dreamed that she spoke to me and asked that I call her Nhan Diep."

"Like in the book you gave me?"

"Yes, that's right. I think the dream quite affected me to begin with," he replied, smiling. "But it was just my mind playing tricks with me. I like the name, though, and it's very appropriate."

"Why's that?"

"Didn't you read the story?"

"Not all of it. I was too tired last night, I'm afraid."

"Oh, that's a shame. It's a delightful tale."

"You mentioned a myth earlier. . . ."

"Yes, well, for a long while," he said, turning in my direction and affording me another look at the red monster, "the Ganges Red held a position in the natural world comparable to that of the yeti or the Loch Ness monster." He chuckled a little. "Until the numerous sightings and testimonies in Zaire there had been a few vague tales of encounters with her. None, however, supplied any supporting proof."

"There's one thing I've been meaning to ask. . . ."

"Hmm?"

"Yes, it's been nagging me since you mentioned Zaire."

"Ah, yes, it's the Democratic Republic of the Congo now. But some people still refer to it as Zaire."

"Oh, yes, I know. That's not what was bothering me. It's about the Ganges river. . . ."

"Yes?"

"Well, it's in India, isn't it?"

"That's right." My host had relaxed considerably since I'd found him wading around in the water earlier on. Perhaps talking about his favorite subject had done it.

"So why is it called the Ganges Red?"

"Well"—Mather faced the tank again—"the first sighting of her, albeit unsubstantiated, was near the city of Varanasi on the left bank of the Ganges over eighteen hundred years ago. There are indications, however, that she was around even before that."

"You mean the species was around then, surely," I tried again, still wondering who he was trying to fool.

"Well, I don't tend to focus too much on the details. After all, this is a myth we're talking about. Myths have been around since the dawn of man, and have always been exaggerated to produce a greater and greater effect. Whether it was the Lady here who was seen eighteen hundred years ago or not, she's still a magnificent specimen."

I let it go. "So, are there any other stories you can tell me?"

"There have been numerous alleged appearances all over the globe. The more modern sightings are the most important ones. In the late nineteenth century she was seen in various locations along the Ganges, but then she seemed to keep out of sight until 1931, when a missionary stationed in Kabalo, in the heart of Zaire, found a small boy washed up on the banks of the Lukuga River with horrific wounds all over his body. The missionary claimed that he himself was then attacked, but luckily left unscathed, by a huge red monster. He was something of an insect specialist, apparently, and despite the size of the creature, he maintained it could be nothing other than a mosquito. The sightings continued, but not with great regularity until recently."

"Right," I said. "But couldn't there still be more Ganges Reds out there?"

"Freaks of nature aren't always unique, it's true. Such accidents can be repeated. However, I have a gut feeling that she may indeed be one of a kind, as amazing as that sounds. As for her life span, well . . . who knows?"

Mather seemed sincere, which bothered me a little. How could he even entertain the notion that this creature had been around for centuries—him being a doctor and man of science? It just didn't make sense. I made up my mind to write the article without any of Mather's wild claims. They would just jeopardize the article's integrity. I would make a reference to it being the only living example of its kind, but I would say nothing of its supposed longevity. After all, a photograph of the thing would be enough to captivate the magazine's readers. There was no need to use myths and legends to decorate the story. I wanted to be thorough, however; I wanted to get as much out of Mather as possible in case I was asked to do a follow-up article. Derek was unpredictable at the best of times. If he asked me to write a second story focusing on the background of the mosquito and the tales it had inspired, it would be good to have the information at hand.

"Tell me more about the legend," I directed.

Without warning, Mr. Hopkins, who was still sitting outside the window, began hissing. His attention was now intensely focused on the mosquito. The cat shrank back from the window, so much so that he nearly fell off the ledge. As he flattened his ears to his head and bared his teeth, I had the strange impression that a battle of wills was taking place between the cat and the insect. I looked from the window back to the recess in the wall, and saw the Ganges Red lift itself off the glass to hover once more above the detritus at the bottom of the tank. The cat maintained its aggressive posture. I was about to say something to Mather, when the animal leaped from the ledge and tore off into the trees.

"So, er . . . the legend?"

"Yes, well, where to start?" Mather sat down on the edge of the bed, crossing his legs and gazing up at the ceiling in concentration. "Among some tribes that live along the Congo river, the Ganges Red is believed to possess more than just a long life span. She is rumored to be immortal. One tribe claims the Ganges Red is a physical manifestation of the Devil."

"The Devil? Whatever next?"

"Yes, quite. There are many variations on this theory, though. Some Indian people who claim to have had contact with her say that rather than actually *being* the Devil, the Ganges Red is more of an instrument, a way for the Prince of Darkness to spread his pain throughout the world. Because of this she earned the title Devil's Hand, which was how she was known until 1962, when Dr. John Harper gave her the name Ganges Red. Harper had spent some time in India and Africa researching a book on abnormal mosquito behavior."

At last I felt the story was moving into the realm of reality. "Do you have a copy of the book?"

"No, I'm afraid not," he said regretfully. "I've tried on numerous occasions to obtain a copy. I must have contacted every specialist bookshop, with no luck. I've been very tempted to look for it in person, but . . . I couldn't leave the island for too long. The Lady here needs constant attention."

"Shame."

"Yes, it is."

"I'll make a point of having a look on the Internet for it when I get back. There are a number of out-of-print book companies I could try."

"That's very good of you." Mather nodded. "Yes, it would be a lovely book to have in my collection. It has an extensive list of the names given to the Ganges Red over the years."

"Really? Do you know any of them?"

"A few. Satan's Claw, Scarlet Death, the Sword of Hell, Hell's Wrath. With some of these names, a little is lost in the translation, but you get the idea."

"How about the Scarlet Woman?" I offered, grinning. "Or the Red Death?"

The look my host returned was hardly one of amusement. "No, I'm afraid not."

Mather sat among his thoughts for a while. I have to admit that the unfolding history of the Ganges Red did interest me. Not only had Mather been telling the truth in his letter, but he'd now presented an intriguing backstory, even if it was far-fetched. The silence continued, and I was about to reach over and press the pause button on the tape recorder, when Mather cleared his throat.

"One story concerns a group of white settlers who encountered the Lady somewhere near the Orange River in South Africa. They were plagued by headaches, fevers and strange dreams for months afterward, even though they hadn't made physical contact with her."

"Headaches?" I asked.

"Yes. Sudden, sharp pains behind their eyes. Most peculiar."

I immediately thought of the stabbing sensation I'd experienced only moments before, then cursed my stupidity. I was being taken in by Mather's story and allowing myself to be spooked.

"Couldn't it have been mass hysteria? A big coincidence?"

"Possibly. Who knows? The group agreed that she was somehow capable of entering their minds, of forcing images into their heads. They said she made them feel apprehensive, paranoid, even terrified."

"How can an insect do that? And why would it, even if it were capable?"

"Perhaps for fun—who knows? Perhaps she was testing her powers. If an insect could manipulate the mind of a man, think what it could do."

"A mosquito with intelligence," I said, smiling. "Now there's a worrying thought."

"Yes." Mather chuckled. "But it makes you wonder. Who are we to say what is and isn't possible? Time turns a lot of assumptions on their head."

"Right. Putting the myth aside for a moment—how does she feed?"

"Ah." His eyebrows lowered as he looked from me to the tank. I followed his gaze and saw that the Ganges Red had concealed itself once more. "Scarlet Death is indeed a fitting label where feeding is concerned.

"A large number of deaths near the Ganges and in locations around Africa have been attributed to the work of our friend here." Mather closed his eyes, perhaps to better see the images in his mind. "What evidence there is suggests the Ganges Red is one of the most effective killers in the natural world." He paused again.

Not for the first time that day I felt uncomfortable. I wanted to separate what Mather was telling me into myth and reality, but it was proving difficult, as he seemed to be blending them together. Was he trying to tell me something? Was he implying that the reality somehow incorporated elements of the myth? I looked again at the tank, more nervous now about its tenant.

"She feeds in much the same way that any female mosquito would, except, because of her size and strength, she is capable of taking in blood at a faster and more efficient rate."

"That would be pretty uncomfortable for the person she's feeding on, wouldn't it? She'd hardly go unnoticed."

"No, indeed." Mather chuckled again. "In fact, it would be impossible for her to go unnoticed. You see, the feeding process causes pain quite unlike the comparatively mild irritation you experience after a bite from a common mosquito. Her smaller relatives inject a natural anesthetic into you, which prevents you from feeling their presence. The Ganges Red doesn't do this. Her saliva, unlike that of other mosquitoes, is highly corrosive. Its effect on human flesh is both devastating and agonizing."

"Jesus," I said, disturbed by the image.

"Yes, the saliva is terribly potent. It immediately begins eating away the tissue surrounding the puncture wound, allowing blood to flow more freely and thereby accelerating the feeding process. The pain is so overwhelming that in less than a minute it can force the victim's body into a state of paralysis. There is, unsurprisingly, no record of anyone surviving a bite. When she has finished the blood meal, she is bloated and will usually rest near the victim until she's in a fit state to fly away. The victim's body, depending on how much saliva she has injected, can be unrecognizable by the time it is discovered."

"Is there any research to back this up? Or is it just part of her legend?"

"Well, I'm just repeating what I've read about her."

"So . . . how do you think she came to be? What could have happened to have produced such an incredible-looking creature?"

"Who can say? If you believe the old legend, then she was born of the ultimate lust. The lust for blood. And not just any blood; the blood of a loved one. Ngoc Tam."

"Didn't he prick himself on a thorn and drip blood onto the body of his wife?"

"He did indeed."

"So what happened after that?"

"Well, Tien Thai, the genie, knew that Ngoc Tam would only find misery if he brought his wife back from the dead—and he was right." Mather crossed and un-crossed his legs. I took his fidgeting as a sign of his obvious enthusiasm for the subject at hand. "Soon after the couple left the genie's island, they came upon a settlement and stopped for supplies. Now," Mather said, holding up one finger, "while Tam was spending the day ashore in the busy markets, buying food, Nhan Diep was taking quite an interest in the large trading ship moored nearby, and its extravagantly dressed captain. By the time Tam returned to his modest raft, Diep and the merchant's vessel were no more than indistinct shapes on the horizon."

"Well," I said, smiling, "it happens every day."

"Ah," Mather replied, "but that's not the end of the story. Eventually, and after great anguish, Tam caught up with the ship and, ignoring the protests of its crew, boarded, demanding to see his wife—"

Suddenly the mosquito started whining loudly and flying about the tank in an agitated manner. Mather slapped his hands on his knees decisively, then stood. "Well now, Mr. Reeves, I fear she may have tired of our attention." He walked back over to the tank. "It might be best to leave her be for a while."

I was left feeling puzzled about the Nhan Diep story, and curious to know its relevance. There were, however, more important questions.

"That stuff about her feeding on people," I said. "It's supposition, isn't it? I mean, you've never seen her do it, have you?"

"Ha," Mather said, still with his back to me. "Of course not. If I had, I'd hardly be alive to talk about it." He was then quiet for what seemed like a long moment, before, with a click of his tongue, he pulled the panel back, covering the recess once more. It slotted into place with an audible click. "As I told you, she sleeps for most of the day. You see, although I feed her regularly, she gets nowhere near the amount of food she would like. In the wild she would take at least one blood meal a day from a large mammal. Birds are her only source of blood here. They seem to suffice, though. She gets one every few days."

"But she eats leaves and stuff as well, doesn't she? Didn't you say earlier that females only feed on blood to aid fertilization?"

Mather was silent again for a few moments. He looked through the window at the dark clouds gathering outside. "For the protein. Yes." He didn't seem particularly focused

81

on the question. Either that or he was debating whether to answer it or not.

"So there's no need to give her blood, is there? I mean, if she really was the only one of her kind left, and the only mosquito of that size, she's unlikely to have any eggs to fertilize."

"That's right," Mather agreed, turning to me and nodding. "No need. But she grows quite agitated if she can't take in blood every now and again. She seems to have a taste for it. . . ."

"Wow. Feeding her must be a pretty risky business. I wouldn't fancy opening that tank, myself."

"No, well, let's just say the Lady and I . . . have an agreement." Something in Mather's voice hinted that he was reluctant to go into further detail on the matter.

"So how do you do it?" I watched Mather as he thought about the question. His left hand tapped his thigh while he stared out of the window.

"I use a little persuasion and a lot of patience." He chuckled to himself. Despite this answer being almost as evasive as the previous one, I decided to drop the matter, sensing that Mather really didn't want to elaborate.

"Well, I think we might leave her to relax a little, hmm?"

"Yes, of course. I think I've got all I need. I'll have to find out the rest of the Nhan Diep story. I'll be doing some more research at the office anyway. Now, if I could take some pictures of her before I go, that would be great."

"No," Mather replied somewhat harshly. "I'm sorry,

excuse me—I'm afraid I can't allow photographs. You see, a story about her is one thing. Your readers can choose to believe it or not. Printing photographs, however, could have serious repercussions. The last thing I want is some lunatic finding the island and trying to get his hands on her."

"I see," I replied, hoping my disappointment wasn't too obvious. I'd been thinking about the photographs throughout the interview. They were crucial, and the story would suffer without them. I didn't want to upset Mather, but at the same time I didn't want to return to the office with nothing but words. "Are you sure I can't take just a couple? I'd hate to lose the story, but I doubt my editor will allow it in the magazine without something visual to go with it. I could always leave out the location of the island from the story."

"I was rather hoping, Mr. Reeves, that you would be doing that anyway." Mather fixed me with a rather serious stare.

"Oh, right. Well, that's no problem, of course."

"Mr. Reeves," he said, looking at the floor, "if the story cannot run without photographs, then I will understand. But please appreciate that I cannot be moved on this issue."

"I understand, really."

"Excellent," he said, brightening. "Then let's move to the living room and discuss the article further." He led me out of the room. I took one last glance at the paneled wall, lamenting the missed opportunity for capturing such an amazing creature on film.

It was a little after nine-thirty and Mather was making another pot of tea. I asked him if coffee was a possibility, but this seemed to bother him, so I changed my mind. It was a shame. I could have done with a stronger caffeine boost. I was still feeling the aftereffects of being in the freezing water the previous day.

Mather looked at the logs in the fireplace as though contemplating a fire. Outside, the sun was covered by oppressive clouds. I took a few sips of tea, imagining it was black coffee. My host looked across at me, his eyes wide open, as though waiting for me to say something. I broke the silence.

"The article . . . ," I said, not intending to finish the sentence.

"Ah, yes," Mather began. "As I was saying, I would prefer it if you didn't give away any revealing details."

"Such as?"

"Well, such as the name of the island, the lake and the town. I would like to remain anonymous too."

The tea made a strange gurgling sound in my stomach. "Anonymous?"

"That's right." He smiled, though it seemed a little forced.

"Well, as I said before, I don't mind keeping certain things confidential. I'm very grateful for the information you've given me. I'm sure it'll be a great story. Although, it would be nice to have real names, real places."

"Well, of course I understand, Mr. Reeves, and sympathize. However, this is a most sensitive case, as I'm sure you've grasped, and precautions must be taken. Otherwise I, as the Lady's guardian, would not be doing my job." He stood, cup in hand, and looked outside. Rays caught his face as the sun broke cover.

"Isn't that better?" Mather drained his cup and set it down on the tray. I was relieved to see him cheerful again. For a while his mood had been a little sour. I was curious about this strange little man, living alone, as he did, on the island with only an oversized mosquito for company. I decided to probe a bit to try to find out more about him.

"You say you studied at Charing Cross Hospital?"

"Yes, that's right," he said, sitting down again.

"That must have been an interesting experience." Perhaps if I showed an interest in his life, he might be more accommodating. I was determined to have photographs of the Ganges Red, even if I had to sneak back into the room at some point to get them. Other people, I'm sure, would have let the matter go, but I knew that if I wanted to be a successful journalist, I'd have to take risks. It was possible that if I remained on the island a little longer, the right opportunity might present itself.

"As a matter of fact," Mather said, "it is because of something that happened during my time there that I came to live here." He scratched his chin and stared into space. "Despite my continued attempts to put the experience behind me, I was driven to flee London and seek the peaceful solitude of Lake Languor."

He looked at the tray, then at my cup, implying that he was keen to clear things away. However, my tea was still hot and, though it wasn't serving any great purpose, I was in no hurry to finish it. Mather settled back in his armchair, staring upward as he recalled the dark tale.

V: ABOMINATION

I took the tape recorder out of my pocket and rested it discreetly on my lap, pressing the record button. I didn't ask Mather for his permission this time, not wanting to interrupt him and risk losing what sounded like a promising story. A lapse in manners is sometimes necessary in my line of work.

"As a young man I lacked the confidence I have now," Mather began. "I allowed myself to be steered by others, and because of this I ended up doing things I didn't want to do. Soames was a man I admired greatly. We met on my first day at medical school in a rather full classroom. I introduced myself, my name coming out in a stutter as it sometimes did when I was nervous. We shook hands.

" 'Soames. Alexander Soames,' he said. There was a remarkable air of self-assurance about him that made me comfortable in his presence. He proceeded to answer every question put to the class by the lecturer, even arguing with the man at one point, much to the class's amusement. I made up my mind to stick to him after that, as he was clearly someone I could learn from. But as I was soon to discover, he was not without his faults. He was prone to sudden and often unexplained fits of rage. Culpability was something he was never able to accept, no matter what evidence there was to implicate him. Nothing was his fault. He would always find some excuse, no matter how flimsy, to lay the blame at another's door. Indeed, if he were here to tell this story himself, he would lay the blame for what happened at *my* door. When he was successful, he would take all the credit and praise, regardless of how many people had helped him. But when things went wrong, he would be quick to accuse others, particularly me."

Mather paused a moment, perhaps for effect, perhaps because the memories were uncomfortable for him.

"The idea came to him while he and I were drinking in our favorite bar near the hospital. Even for someone training to be a surgeon, Soames had an amazing pre-occupation with anatomy. He believed that secrets could be revealed through new and unorthodox forms of anatomical study. A great number of his theories came from dreams he'd had, a worrying fact on its own, but even more worrying when on occasion he would actually carry out the bizarre experiments suggested by his subconscious.

"It seemed a natural thing to him to spend most of his spare time among the bodies in the morgue, dissecting, examining, looking for heaven knows what. The other students, and a number of the doctors, gave Soames a wide berth. To them he was something of a monster. In appearance he was tall and thin and had long, black, unwashed hair that stuck to his forehead in greasy, unflattering clumps. He towered above me and had a stride that often left me far behind, struggling to keep up. How Soames bought his clothes I don't know, but they were poorly chosen. His shirts were too small, his trousers too short. Fashion didn't appear to interest him; like so many other things it was a distraction from his work. Sometimes he would spend entire nights doing things that the rest of us students would try to avoid, unless it was part of our coursework. Many were the stories we heard of poor unsuspecting nurses stumbling upon the dirty, exhausted figure of Soames, hunched over a corpse in the morgue, doing all sorts of horrible things to it. Oh, he never did anything illegal or perverted, as far as I am aware, but his enthusiasm was, shall we say, excessive.

"But the dark and deeply regrettable incident that led to Soames and me parting ways involved a particularly gruesome dream he'd had about what he described as 'unwarranted organ extraction.' Panting with excitement, he told me that the exact organ to be removed wasn't important, it was the effects of the removal that he was interested in. It had to be an organ with an important function. That way the results of the extraction would be clearly and immediately apparent.

"On hearing Soames's idea I was horrified, and remain so to this day. I had to ask him to repeat what he'd told me, so I could be sure I hadn't misheard. He went over it again, this time in slow, careful detail. I sat for a while in stunned silence, until Soames demanded to know what was troubling me.

"That he had to ask made me laugh out loud. How

could he not see that what he proposed went beyond the unethical and into the realms of the inhuman? I tried without success to change his mind. In his eyes that night I could almost glimpse a growing madness fueled by an insatiable curiosity. I had the feeling that he was keeping something from me—perhaps something even more outrageous than what he'd already divulged—because he knew what I'd say or do if I found out.

"I repeatedly made objections to Soames's plan. I tried in vain to assure him that, quite apart from the moral issue, such a procedure was fraught with complications. As a medical student I had a responsibility to preserve life where possible—to avoid inflicting unnecessary pain and torture. I could not allow myself to take part in such foul schemes. Soames sighed when he learned that my answer was no, and realized that he should stop trying to convince me. He seemed more somber than angry, and resigned himself to tackling his work alone.

"The next day the only thing on my mind was Soames's plan. Without supervision of some kind he would be free to do whatever he wished, and that disturbed me. I convinced myself that I'd have to pretend to agree to assist him, purely to be in a position of control, to stop him from going too far. That night I approached him in the bar under the pretense that I had come round to his way of thinking. A weight of depression seemed to lift from him immediately and he dashed away to buy drinks. What I was doing was dangerous, and I prayed I had made the right decision. Soames sloshed and spilled the beer in his rush to get it back to the table. The cuffs of his gray shirt were soaking by the time he sat down.

" 'Excellent,' he said, a fire in his eyes. 'This is very good news. I was dreading the idea of working alone. You don't know how much this means to me.'

" 'Well,' I said, faking a grin, 'I knew you'd do it anyway and I reckon things will go a lot more smoothly if I'm there to lend a hand.'

" 'They will indeed,' Soames enthused. 'They will indeed!'

" 'But tell me, where are you going to find someone who'll let you operate on them in this way?'

" 'You leave that to me, my friend. You'll be surprised how many willing subjects there are out there, prepared to do all sorts of things for next to nothing.'

" 'Like who?'

" 'Who? Have you looked in the gutter recently? In shop doorways?'

" 'The homeless?'

" 'Yes, the "homeless." My dear boy, some of these people are all but screaming to take part in such endeavors. They are the desperate, the addicted. They operate on a different level from you and me. A lower level. Their needs are simpler, their demands less expensive.'

" 'You will be careful, though? I mean, you'll treat them with respect? The respect—'

" 'That any human being would demand? Of course. I am human, after all.'

" 'You must ensure that you don't inflict any long-term

damage on the patients,' I said, adopting a serious tone. 'What you'll be doing subverts lawful medical practice.'

" 'Yes, yes,' Soames said. 'But what doesn't these days? Sometimes bending the rules is the only way to make progress. But don't worry, I'll ensure that no one finds out.'

" 'How, exactly?'

" 'Oh, I'm a man of resource. I'm always careful to keep prying eyes away from my business.'

" 'Soames—'

" 'Just relax, will you? Trust me. What we're about to embark on is a quest of discovery and enlightenment. I'm doing this in the name of medicine, to benefit my fellow man.'

" 'Are you?'

" 'Oh, Mather, for heaven's sake!' Soames paused for a while to think something over. 'I'm not a monster.'

" 'I know, but—'

" 'Believe me, I'd know if I were going too far.' He took a few mouthfuls of beer. I think I'd relaxed a little by now, but I still wasn't wholly convinced of Soames's assertions. His past behavior suggested that he didn't know what 'too far' was, and didn't care either.

" 'Come on, drink up,' he encouraged. 'I'll get another round.'

"We ended up quite drunk that night. I cheered up considerably as the evening went on, but I was beginning to doubt my ability to stop Soames's diabolical project. I wish things had been different.

"Just before closing time we left the bar and walked to the bus stop, where Soames caught his bus home. I lived in the student quarters by the hospital, a situation I had long preferred. Living among other people had always suited me. Just hearing voices through the walls of my room was comforting. Since then, as you can tell, my preference has altered drastically. Soames, on the other hand, thrived on isolation. The large house he rented must have cost him a pretty penny, but he had lost his parents at a young age and had been brought up by a wealthy aunt. I guessed that she must have provided her nephew with some sort of subsidy. He hardly mentioned her, but based on the rare occasions she did crop up in conversation I had the impression that she was a strict, coldhearted woman, and that Soames was glad to be free of her. He would rarely invite me or anyone else back to his house. I think it was an important refuge for him.

"I was surprised when, the next day, Soames told me he was ready to conduct his experiment. There were dark bags under his eyes. He'd been having trouble sleeping. Either that, or he'd been preparing for the experiment all night. Whichever was the case, I was consumed by a great unease. I lied and told him I had arranged to be somewhere else. My story crumbled, however, under an unprecedented interrogation. Soames managed to work his way around every excuse I gave him until I finally relented. His determination seemed so set that nothing could get in his way.

"The night came fast. I was tempted to go to the bar

and get a few drinks inside me for courage, but such an idea might have been disastrous. Unpleasant questions kept running through my mind. Who would he find to be the subject for the experiment? How would he ensure that they survived? What if the worst happened and the subject died? Would he be guilty of murder? One thing I was sure of: if Soames was to be kept under control, I would have to stay sober, so I decided against going to the bar. I arrived at his house at eleven o'clock in the evening, as arranged, and knocked on the door. Not a sound came from inside the house. My hands ran trembling through my hair.

" 'Maybe he started without me,' I said aloud. Stepping back, I looked up at the first-floor windows. There were no lights on in the house. I was puzzled. Knowing how precise and clinical Soames was, I thought there had to be something seriously wrong for him to have missed the appointment. I waited for some minutes, wondering if my watch was wrong. Then Soames appeared at the gate behind me. He strode up the path, one hand holding something in a brown paper bag, the other fumbling in his pocket for his keys.

" 'Sorry to keep you waiting. I had to pop out for five minutes,' he said, grinning and pushing the key into the lock. 'All is set, though. I can't wait to get started.' He opened the door and I followed him inside.

"The interior of the house suggested that Soames wasn't house-proud. The walls of the living room were covered in old beige wallpaper, whole sheets of which were peeling off in places. There was a small sofa and an armchair that had both seen better days, and the fireplace had been sealed up and painted over. There was no television or radio, not even a lamp or ornament of any description. It was obviously a room he spent little time in. I lowered myself slowly into the cushioned grasp of the armchair, in case it fell apart. Soames insisted on making me a cup of coffee, which he went to the kitchen to prepare.

"I looked at the peeling walls. There was an odd feeling in my stomach. My mouth was dry, my palms were sweating. I wanted to get on with the matter in hand. The longer I waited, the more my imagination ran wild. A short while later Soames brought in a large mug of coffee for me, then left, muttering to himself. The first sip scalded my tongue, making me curse aloud. When the liquid had cooled I took a second sip, but when it hit my stomach, I immediately felt ill. Just then Soames returned and diverted my attention from the growing nausea within me.

"He appeared in the doorway wearing a surgical gown and carrying a second one for me. 'Here you go,' he said, passing me the white garment. 'Drink up and we'll begin.'

"I didn't feel like finishing the coffee, but under his gaze I felt compelled to do so. The liquid gurgled and sloshed around in my gut, unwilling to settle, as though it were an unwelcome guest. I placed the mug on the floor and dressed myself in the gown. Soames then led me out into the corridor and up the stairs to the first floor. Across the landing he opened the door to a large bedroom and welcomed me inside.

"The first thing I noticed on entering the room was the amount of light. It was incredibly bright in there. The curtains were closed, and in addition to the light on the ceiling Soames had arranged three electric lamps around the room. They must have been fitted with the most powerful bulbs available, as they rendered the room all but devoid of shadow. Once I'd grown semiaccustomed to the glare, I noticed the man lying unconscious on the table.

"He was a tramp. There could be no doubt about that. His clothes were old, torn and badly stained. He was un-shaven and the back of his neck was dark with dirt, his hair tangled and matted. I glanced at Soames, who merely smiled and clapped me on the back.

" 'Right!' He went over to a smaller table on which he had arranged a collection of surgical implements. 'Shall we?'

" 'Is he asleep?'

" 'No, but he's deeply inebriated. Trust me, he won't flinch. I've just bought another bottle of Scotch in case he requires further sedation. I would use anesthetic, but I couldn't get any from the hospital. They guard that stuff so well you'd think it was gold bullion. Still, one must learn to improvise.' I looked at the brown paper bag on the floor, and the bottle of Scotch that had been in it. The cap had been screwed off, ready for use. 'Right, help me turn him onto his back.'

" 'Wait a minute,' I said, feeling more unwell. 'Are you sure you know what you're doing?'

" 'I'm positive. For God's sake, man, have more faith.'

" 'I still think this is a really bad idea,' I said.

"Soames looked at me as though I were mad. 'My good friend, what on earth is the matter? There's nothing to be frightened of.'

" 'I'm not frightened!' It was a lie. My whole body felt unnaturally cold.

" 'It's OK'—he put a hand on my shoulder—'I promise you. It'll be fine.'

" 'OK. So . . .' I tried to look calmer than I actually was. 'You're going to remove the liver, record the effects on his body, then reattach it?'

" 'Yes, that's it.' I detected a little hesitation in Soames's response. Something wasn't right. 'Like I said the other day, it's an unwarranted organ extraction. The liver is an essential organ, so removing it will produce obvious results. I'll record those results and later analyze them. Grab his legs, would you?'

" 'And how exactly will science benefit from this?'

"He sighed. 'Well, if we can see how the body reacts to losing its essential organs, we may be able to find ways of compensating for such loss. For example, the absence of the liver will result in the rapid onset of blood poisoning. If we are able to accurately record this, then we can come up with alternative methods of blood purification, or even preventative measures—'

" 'But that's basic medicine,' I interrupted. 'Anyone

97

with a rudimentary knowledge of anatomy could come to that conclusion. I've seen people with liver failure and jaundice. It's not pleasant, but everyone understands what's happening.'

" 'Yes . . . but those people are treated, they are made as comfortable as possible—they are not thoroughly studied. I intend to take that important step, to analyze the process from beginning to end, like no one has done before.' Soames looked down at the subject on the table. 'I doubt this fellow's liver would have served him much longer, anyway.'

" 'Yes, but you *are* going to reattach it, aren't you? Regardless of its condition?'

" 'Oh, come on,' Soames replied calmly. 'He's all but destroyed himself with alcohol. He could go at any time— look at him.'

" 'I really hope you're not implying what I think—'

" 'Oh, don't be dense, man!' Soames's explosive outburst surprised me. 'Look, if it had been someone a little healthier, then maybe I could have restored the organ after a brief period, but I can't begin to think of the difficulty involved in securing a willing, healthy subject. Listen, I spoke to him at great length and explained everything. He's consented fully to—'

" 'What? His death?'

" 'Well . . . yes. We can't just throw away this golden opportunity—'

" 'No! No way, Soames. This is wrong, this is very, very wrong. You can't just bloody kill the man!'

" 'Oh, what could he possibly have to live for? Let him make a contribution to medical science and give his pathetic life some meaning. I don't understand why you're trying to make this sound so macabre all of a sudden.'

" 'Because it is! It's murder!'

" 'Is it? Is it murder if he's consented? Is it murder if it leads to a valuable discovery? A discovery that could at some point save lives?'

" 'That's speculation! You're in no position to play with people's lives—to play God!'

"Soames fixed my gaze then, as though trying to communicate something with his eyes that words couldn't. He smiled. 'Mather, my dear friend . . . we *are* gods.'

"I felt my lips tremble, as though in readiness for a reply, but none was forthcoming. I had no answer to that. It was quite a while, in fact, before I was able to say anything.

" 'It was my understanding that you'd remove the organ, record the results, then put it back.'

"Soames pursed his lips, looked down at the floor and, to my amazement, laughed. 'Poor, poor Mather. God bless you. You really think it's possible to take out the liver and put it back after what could be several minutes of separation? Your naïveté is almost charming. Tell me, how exactly did you think I'd ensure life support during such a procedure? I was lucky to get these,' he said, gesturing at his instruments.

" 'You bastard! I'm not going to let you do this,' I spat. 'I can't allow it!'

" 'What do you mean, you can't allow it?' He was angry now. 'Just who do you think you are?'

" 'I'm not going to let you murder this man. What did you expect to do if the university found out, or the police . . . ?'

" 'Let me deal with them. You came here to assist. This procedure is my responsibility. Now help me move him, would you?'

" 'No. I won't.'

" 'I see.' Soames stood looking at me. He tapped his foot on the floor. 'If you don't help me now, I promise I'll go through with this experiment anyway, and—'

" 'No, you won't—'

" 'Oh, yes, I will! You can't watch me every hour of the day, Mather. I'll do it. And if it goes wrong, I'll frame you. How will that look? Hmm? And who would the university believe? Me with my exemplary grades? Or you with your mediocre performance?'

" 'You'd be taking a big gamble.'

" 'Maybe. But I'm cleverer than you are. If I want to frame you, I will. You know that. If you want a positive conclusion to this matter, your only hope is to assist me.'

" 'I would be an accomplice to murder.'

" 'Stop saying that! It's not murder!' Soames glared at me. 'As I said before, he has consented.' He sniffed and looked at the patient. 'Now, I need a steady hand and complete silence to work. If you're not going to help me, perhaps you should leave.' With a great effort he shifted the man onto his back by himself, then ripped open his shirt. I caught the unpleasant stench of stale sweat. Standing immobile and indecisive, I watched while Soames shaved the man's torso and prepared the area with iodine. Finishing, he reached for a scalpel.

"Finally breaking my shock-induced stupor, I walked up to Soames and grabbed his hand.

" 'Get off me,' he spat in disgust. 'What do you think you're doing?'

" 'Drop it, Soames. Drop it now, or I'll go straight to the police.'

" 'Will you indeed? I'm sure they'd be interested in the part you've played in this matter.' I hesitated for a moment. It was long enough for him to shake his hand free and turn his attention back to the patient. 'The police!' he sneered. 'You'll do no such thing.'

" 'I'm serious,' I threatened.

" 'So am I. You're as much a part of this as I am. You wouldn't dare involve the police.'

" 'I came here to stop you making a big mistake. I thought I could make you see sense. If I'd known you weren't intending to reattach the organ, I'd have probably had you arrested by now. If this man dies, you'll be a murderer. You're my friend, for Christ's sake . . . do you think I want to see you go to prison?'

"I thought I might break Soames. The hand holding the scalpel began to tremble slightly. He stood over the patient for quite some time, creating an awkward silence that made me wonder if he'd entered some sort of trance. Then, quietly but purposefully, he placed the scalpel back on the metal tray and wiped his damp brow with the front of a shirtsleeve.

" 'Very well,' he said, disappointed. 'Leave me alone for a while, would you? I'll sober him up and sort him out.'

"It's bizarre, but I almost felt sorry for Soames. His face, as I left the room, was a portrait of defeat. I wanted to say something, but couldn't. He had the bearing of a man who'd been thwarted on the brink of something magnificent. I departed without a word. There was nothing to say.

"Downstairs I made myself a cup of tea. Taking the drink into the living room, I reclined on the sofa. I took one careful sip and then put the mug down. The tea tasted good and it calmed me somewhat after the heated exchange. I pictured Soames in the room above, perhaps muttering under his breath and cursing my name while he revived the patient. My eyelids drooped and my breathing grew loud and regular. Feeling drained, I allowed myself to sleep.

"I awoke a little while later, in the grip of a sudden panic. There was a wealth of noise from the room above. Amid desperate shouts from Soames, I could hear the muffled screams of a creature in great pain and distress. It didn't take me long to guess what must be occurring up there. I jumped off the sofa, left the room and took the stairs two at a time. Before reaching the room I heard Soames cry, 'Oh . . . oh, Jesus!'

"The theater was a mess. Medical instruments were strewn across the floorboards and the whisky bottle had been smashed, leaving a large section of the floor dark and wet. Soames flinched at the sound of my arrival and turned to face me. Blood and horror were splashed across his face. Approaching him, I saw the mangled form of the vagrant sprawled across the floor, limbs twisted in unnatural shapes, his whole body shaking uncontrollably.

"Words cannot adequately convey the awfulness of what confronted me. Perhaps it will suffice to say that I could never have imagined that a human being, or any animal, could be so wholly consumed by pain.

" 'Oh dear,' Soames said, quite insufficiently.

"I tried to avoid watching the tramp's horrible convulsions, but it proved impossible.

" 'Can't we do something?' I pleaded.

" 'Like what? His liver's gone,' Soames replied. And then, in a tone at once cold and devoid of emotion: 'He's dying.'

"I felt a sudden anger. My so-called friend had lied to me. He'd never intended to abort the operation. There was not a trace of compassion in his heart. In his eyes I saw a fire that burned for more than mere knowledge. There was something lustful and hateful there.

"I had failed to stop Soames, and because of this I felt partly responsible for his act of brutality. It was a testament to his deviousness and tenacity that he'd managed to complete his atrocious task.

103

"Inevitably, the homeless man died. His death, I am sad to say, was neither quick nor painless. I begged Soames to end the suffering, but he insisted on leaving the man alone, to fully record the results of the abominable experiment.

"I felt unable to move until the man had finally expired. Soames pleaded with me to remain. He insisted he needed my assistance in cataloging the findings. I think what he really wanted was my help in disposing of the body, but I would have nothing more to do with the matter. He could clean up his own mess.

"That evening the nightmares began. Even during the days following, I could see the poor wretch's face painted in a permanent mask of horror and hear his agonized screams. He has never left my thoughts since. Much as I had expected, Soames kept his distance from me after that night. I only saw him at classes, where he would sit all alone at the back of the room, trying when possible to tackle all practical assignments by himself.

"About a month or so after the incident Soames disappeared. No one knew where he had gone, or why, but in the months before he vanished rumors had circulated of disappearances in the area. Perhaps Soames had continued his experiments without my help. I dread to think what he might have done.

"When I became a practicing surgeon I thought I would be able to put it all behind me, but my career seemed tainted from the beginning. Every operation I performed brought back that memory as clear as day. Somehow I managed to work for sixteen years before the memories and guilt threw me into a state of depression and despair."

Mather paused, the story clearly dredging up old, unwelcome emotions. I sat quietly for some moments, trying to process what he had told me. I think it goes without saying that it isn't every day I hear a story like that. I tried to imagine myself in Mather's position. The idea was horrific. Perhaps he was unaware of how shocking and frightening such a story would be to a stranger like myself. He sipped his tea and stared out of the window. The odd cloud came and went, casting gray shadows across his face.

"Luckily, I'd saved a considerable sum of money, and was able to move here," Mather continued. "I could finally pursue my real obsession—the Lady."

I looked at the tape recorder to see if there was still enough tape left. It had almost reached the end of one side, but Mather's story seemed to be coming to a close. I couldn't help but feel uneasy. Why had he told me all this? And why had he been so honest about not trying to stop Soames earlier? He hadn't struck me as the sort of person who would be intimidated easily. Why hadn't he gone to the police at the earliest opportunity? Surely he would have, if he'd been truly appalled at what his friend had done. I was beginning to worry about the sort of person Mather might be.

"Everything I've done until now feels justified because of her," he said.

"Right," I replied, nodding. "That's a pretty bleak story, though, isn't it? It must be a hard thing to live with."

"It is. That's why I'm better off being here. It keeps me away from the horrors of society, the reminders. And the Lady is such good company." He smiled.

"Aren't you at all worried that she might escape, though? I mean, wouldn't she attack you just as she would anyone?"

"Maybe," Mather answered in an almost detached manner. "It depends . . ."

"On what?" I looked at Mather as he stood and walked over to the living room window.

"Looks like it's clearing up again." He was right. The dark clouds had passed, and over the lake the glorious sun presided. Mather picked up my cup and placed it on the tray with his. He left without a word and went into the kitchen.

I thought about what I'd asked him and why he hadn't answered. Glancing outside again, I decided, if Mather had no objection, to go for another walk before he took me back to the mainland. After the story I'd just heard I needed some fresh air and time alone. And if he'd let me I wanted to take some photographs of the house and its surroundings. Leaving the living room, I went to my room to retrieve my bag. On the way I noticed that no sound was coming from the kitchen. Whatever Mather was doing, he was doing it in silence. I thought about going into his bedroom to get some pictures of the Ganges Red. Would he catch me? If he did, what would he do?

No, I would wait. I was already spooked by his story, and by him. I had no idea how he'd react if he caught me betraying his wishes. But if I could get him away from the house, maybe then I would have the opportunity I needed.

VI: REVELATION

Mather was deep in thought when I joined him in the kitchen. He was washing the crockery, but doing so in a curiously slow manner. I was about to ask if anything was wrong when, on seeing me standing in the doorway, he started, almost dropping the cup he was holding.

"Sorry," I said. "I didn't mean to creep up on you."

"No, it's my fault, really. I was preoccupied for a moment. . . ." He looked embarrassed, though I couldn't think why. "Oh," he said, noticing that my bag was slung around my shoulder, "are you leaving already?"

"In a short while, yes. So much work to do back at the office, you know. But I wouldn't mind having another quick look around the island before I go."

"Oh, well, let me finish this and I'll come with you."

"Oh, no, that's very kind of you, but I'd rather go alone, if you don't mind. I wanted to get some photographs of the house and the lake for the article—if that's OK with you?"

"Oh, well now, I don't—"

"Obviously I understand what you said earlier, about not wanting people coming to the island, but I'll only use general shots of trees and the lake. Nothing revealing."

"You give me your word?"

"Absolutely."

"Well . . . all right, then. I'll leave you to it. But remember, I don't want any names mentioned in the article. I'm very sensitive about that sort of thing."

"No, I realize that. Don't worry, I'll be back in about half an hour or so. Then we can go, if that's all right?"

"That's fine."

"Great." I smiled and turned while Mather remained by the sink as though waiting for me to leave. "Right, I'll be off then. See you in a while."

Just as I left Mather said, "Be careful not to go too far down the path—it's not safe past the boathouse. All sorts of thorn bushes. I never go near that side of the island as a rule."

"Oh, right—OK, I'll be careful."

Outside, the air was fresh and pleasant. A movement caught my eye, and on looking back at the house I saw the curtains at the living room window twitch. Stepping back a few paces, almost to the tree line, I took my camera out of the bag and checked it was in working order. Everything was as it should be, so I took a few pictures of the house from various angles, then returned the camera to the bag. I wondered again how Mather survived on his own. There couldn't be many people prepared to live in such isolation. Was his experience with Soames the sole reason for such a drastic decision? The mental aspect of his situation was intriguing. I could be a solitary person myself a lot of the time, but it was hard to imagine getting by without regular social interaction. I'd go insane. Maybe we don't realize how dependent we are on others until we are truly detached. From what I had seen, though, Mather seemed to cope with his detachment pretty well.

I walked toward the beach, then changed my mind. There was little more of interest in that direction, and I was sure there would be better views of the lake from elsewhere on the island. I set off along the path I'd discovered earlier. Luckily, many of the branches had been moved safely out of the way during my previous excursion, so my progress was easier. It didn't take long to reach the rocks above the second beach. Taking out the camera and looping the strap over my neck, I looked through the viewfinder at the lake beyond. It was shaping up to be a really good day. There were a few puffs of cloud, but they were stretched thin across the sky. The surface of the lake glimmered brilliantly in the morning sun. There could be no starker contrast to the day before. I took a few exposures of the wide expanse, then moved on, this time leaving the camera hanging around my neck.

The path ended by the rocks. Beside the beach and the boathouse there was only dense undergrowth. However, while turning back down the path, I noticed a small gap in the trees. Mather had warned me about going in that direction, but perhaps he was being overanxious. I walked up to the small gap and looked around. All that could be seen was nettles and branches. Tucking my hands into my pockets, I proceeded carefully forward.

I had to push with some force to begin with, but after shouldering aside several branches I found that the new path wasn't too different from the previous one. It snaked toward the opposite end of the island, so I started off eagerly.

There were birds in the trees around me, but I was unable to see them. So far, all the photos I'd taken were of the house and the lake. I wanted to get some of the local wildlife on film, in case I was ultimately unable to photograph the Ganges Red. Continuing down the path, I caught a glimpse of the back of Mather's house. As I moved into the trees to find a better position, I was soon rewarded. There was a window at the end of the corridor which was curtained on the inside. Below this was a small wooden hut, a little bigger than a kennel, which must have housed the generator. Although Mather had said he didn't use much electricity, the machine must have been important to him. I tried to imagine myself being stranded on the island at night with nothing but candles to get me around. It wasn't a comforting thought.

The view of the house and generator was creepy enough to give the article the right atmosphere. I reeled off a few frames through the branches, the clicks disturbing some of the birds nearby. When I was happy, I returned to the path and continued walking.

The chirping of the birds soon grew distant, as though they weren't interested in this part of the island anymore. The path widened, narrowed and almost disappeared in places as I made my way along it, whistling the odd tune or just listening to the sound of the branches swaying in the wind. As I walked on, I wondered if there would be anything of interest at the end of the path.

LAKE LANGUOR RESEARCH CENTER
ARIES ISLAND
NO TRESPASSING

The sign hung slightly askew on the gate that crossed the path, and despite the faded lettering it grabbed my attention. I was immediately faced by a rather worrying question. Why had Mather told me there were no other buildings? He'd said that he didn't come to this side of the island much, but I found it hard to believe that he knew nothing of the research center.

I stood staring at the sign for a while, momentarily unable to proceed. It was those two simple yet powerful words: NO TRESPASSING. I took a couple of photographs, then walked up to the gate. It seemed odd that a research center should be at the end of such a rarely used trail. Even if it had been closed down for a while, I'd have expected more than just a rough path. Perhaps there was a second approach to the center from another beach. I scanned the trees around me nervously for signs of movement, but didn't really expect to see anyone watching. Climbing onto the gate, I swung my legs over and dropped to the ground on the other side. The path continued beyond the gate and round to the left.

Turning the corner, I saw a brick building a short way in front of me. It was undoubtedly deserted. Time and the seasons had taken their toll on the place, and the thick foliage on all sides was slowly trying to smother it. I lifted the camera and moved back slightly to fit the building in the frame. Just then a small rabbit hopped out of the bushes some meters ahead and sat there, its head tilted quizzically toward me. I took the picture with the animal in the foreground. The rabbit, surprised at the sound, turned and hopped back into the trees. I lowered the camera and looked again at the building. It wasn't even a mile from the house. How could Mather not know of its existence?

I could see no evidence from the outside of what research had been carried out in there. On approaching the porch, however, I saw a small plaque on the brickwork to the left of the door.

LAKE LANGUOR MARINE RESEARCH CENTER

Thick, lustrous ivy twisted its way up the wooden pillars that supported the porch roof. The front door was glass from the middle up. This had browned from moisture and dirt that must have collected over several years. The lower part of the door was warped and rotting. Some white paint still remained in places, but most of it had flaked off long ago. I reached for the knob, which turned easily. Pushing the door open and stepping inside, I was immediately assailed by the smell of decaying wood, damp vegetation and something else. It was like the terrible smell of rotting food, only worse.

The room I entered was a small reception area that had been gutted. Where once a few chairs had been bolted to the ground, there were now just holes. To the right, on the floor, were the many shards of a broken vase, green now with filth. A page from a magazine, almost bleached white by time, had imprinted itself on the linoleum like an accidental tattoo.

I walked through the small foyer and into a large, light room that must once have been a laboratory. The smell was stronger now, and ignoring it was proving difficult. My shoes crunched on broken glass. Green light from the leaves covering one window highlighted a number of large, aquarium-style tanks along the right wall, some intact, some in various stages of destruction. In front of these were high tables, covered in dirt and debris. I assumed that it was here that the staff had conducted their experiments. As I walked down the center of the room, I saw that a stool had been smashed into one of the tanks. It had clearly been an act of vandalism, but who would do such a thing? And was it done before or after Mather came to the island?

At the end of the room were two doors. The first, on the left, led to an annex, where I found what looked like a staff room, toilets and a fair-sized storage cupboard. In the staff room I noticed an old science magazine not unlike *Missing Link* lying on the floor, kicked into one corner. I stood over it and peered down. It lay open at a story on termite infestation, and rare breeds of so-called super termites. Someone was obviously interested in the authors of the article, Pat Harold and C. H. Peters, as they had circled the names with a marker. Leaving the filthy magazine where it was, I returned to the main room and tried the other door.

I turned the handle and pushed inward, but the door budged only slightly. It seemed to be wedged against the frame. I had to give it a good strong kick to force a gap wide enough for me to squeeze through.

Finding myself at the top of some concrete steps, I looked around for a light switch, then realized that the generator, wherever it was, would probably be inactive. The smell was much worse now, and I felt I could almost touch it as it wafted up the stairs from below. Despite the possible dangers, the journalist in me was determined to discover what was down there in the gloom.

Not having a flashlight with me, I went back into the main room where there was natural light and took the camera flash out of the bag. Luckily, like the camera it-self, it hadn't been affected by the previous day's soaking. I attached it to the flash housing and waited for it to warm up before taking a test shot. There were only two more exposures left on the film, so there seemed little point in removing it. I returned to the door and was able to descend half the staircase before needing to use the camera. Snapping off the first flash, I saw the lower half of the stairs, and made my way down in the darkness, retaining the afterimage in my head.

I reached the foot of the stairs and set off another flash. This time the light revealed a small basement, with shelves and boxes stacked on top of each other. On a small table in one corner I was sure I'd glimpsed an oil lamp. Closing my eyes, I studied the image burned onto my retinas. There was definitely something in that direction. I walked over and aimed the flash down at the spot in question. There was indeed an oil lamp, along with a large box of kitchen matches to one side of it.

"Result," I muttered to myself. I felt for the box, struck a match, and then picked up the lamp, unsure how to light the thing. The match had burned dangerously close to my fingers by the time the lamp was lit. I held it up, illuminating the basement. The only thing I'd missed when I glimpsed it with the flash was the door by the bottom of the stairs. Pocketing the matches, I looked around the shelves and boxes for anything else of interest. Finding nothing, I turned my attention to the door.

There was no doorknob this time, so I just pushed the door and found that it opened inward with little encouragement. Holding up the lamp, I found a slightly larger room than the one before. The floor was black: for some reason it seemed to have been painted, though clumsily, as some light patches showed through. Holes had been drilled in a number of locations, though for what purpose I couldn't fathom. There was a large table in the middle of the room, also painted—something which struck me as particularly odd. Waving the lantern around the walls, I saw a couple of small shelves and a chest of drawers. I counted at least seven oil lamps, placed at various points around the room, no doubt in an attempt to illuminate the whole area for work of some kind. As well as the now horrible smell of spoiled food there was a strange smell of rust coming from somewhere. I angled the lamp toward the floor. In some places the light penetrated part of the way through the strange paint, revealing its layers. I was beginning to feel ill, and not just from the smell. It felt as if my subconscious were trying to tell me something that I didn't want to hear.

There was an open doorway at the opposite end of this room, and I decided to check it out before I was totally overcome by the foul air.

I was very lucky not to have walked straight through, as there was a sudden drop into some kind of pit. The opposite wall was a couple of meters away, but I couldn't tell how far down the floor was. Kneeling on the threshold, holding the lamp low and nearly retching now at the fumes assaulting my nostrils, I could make out various shapes some way below. I waved the lantern back and forth, but couldn't make any sense of what was down there.

Stepping back from the ledge, I took the camera from over my shoulder and put it down on the floor to my right so that it wouldn't get in my way. I lit one of the other lamps, so I now had two, and took them both back to the edge of the pit. Setting one down carefully behind me and to my right, I lay down on the floor and dangled the other into the darkness. I swung the lamp about but still couldn't understand what I was seeing. Deciding there was nothing else to do, I took off my belt, looped one end around the handle of the lamp, securing it tightly through the buckle, then lowered it over the edge. I let the lamp drop lower and lower until, in a moment of clumsiness, I lost my grip on the belt. The lamp dropped onto the huge pile at the bottom of the pit. Squinting, I could make out a familiar object, now illuminated by the lamp, which had landed upright. I gasped, forgetting for a split second the stench that surrounded me.

"Oh, God," I uttered in a voice barely recognizable as my own. Frozen in a claw of death was a hand, jutting from a tangled heap of bodies, some clothed, some not, all in various stages of decomposition. Shivering suddenly, and finding it hard to draw a breath, I got to my feet and stood, staring down at the horror below. Just then something in the room behind me clattered to the floor. My whole body jerked in reaction to the sound and I lost my balance, falling forward, hopelessly, into the open grave.

VII: DESPERATION

I plunged headfirst into the mound of corpses. Luckily, I had my arms in front of me to soften the impact, but I was still left dazed. In my fall I had kicked over the lamp by the doorway, in addition to the lamp in the pit, so that I was in darkness. As I pushed myself onto my elbows, I felt something soft and wet yield beneath me. I slowly turned and sat up, not wanting the pile to collapse. The smell was nauseating now, and each breath brought me closer to madness. Keeping the food in my gut was an ordeal. The smell was in my lungs, my throat, my sinuses, everywhere. I tried slowing my breathing, but the only result was an oxygen deficit, which I had to compensate for by gulping down huge mouthfuls of the detestable air.

My right foot started to slip between two bodies, so I shifted my position to avoid being sucked down. The noise I'd heard could have been made by someone in the room above, but all was silent now; there was no reaction to my heavy, desperate breathing. The lamp, which had been between my legs, slipped from its position and fell forward slightly. In the gloom around me I could see nothing but indistinct shapes of black and gray. I took the box of matches from my pocket and relit the lamp. It looked as if there were at least two dozen bodies in the pile beneath me.

My breathing calmed as I sat there, unable to tear my gaze from the doorway, waiting for Mather's silhouette to appear at any second. Why hadn't he approached the hole? Why wasn't he coming to kill me? Surely that was what he intended to do now? I began muttering under my breath, praying perhaps, begging for someone to deliver me from the horrifying mess I'd landed myself in. Time passed, and I was beginning to wonder what the hell he was doing, when I heard a sneeze, then a strange rasping noise. I tensed, waiting for something terrible to happen, then at last a dark shape appeared in the doorway.

Mr. Hopkins scanned the mound of bodies below him, as though looking for the quickest way down. His sense of smell must have been way more advanced than mine, so I couldn't understand why he wanted to get closer to all that dead flesh. He uttered a long, indulgent meow, then walked along the length of the doorway, as if trying to find a better way to join me. Giving up, he lowered his whole body, then stretched his front legs over the edge, so that his paws were against the wall. He kept moving until he began to slip, then tensed himself for the fall. He landed softly and without any noticeable discomfort to my right, on the back of a large body wrapped in dirty sheets.

"Hello," I said, my voice rougher and drier than I had

expected. Mr. Hopkins meowed again in reply, then started rubbing his body against my legs. "You could have picked a better moment. But at least it's you and not that madman. What the hell is going on here?" Mr. Hopkins stopped prowling around and lay down next to me, purring softly. I shook my head and looked back up at the doorway. It was possible for me to reach the ledge, but it would be difficult. The cat just lay there purring and blinking at me. Maybe he had no sense of smell at all. I moved into a crouch, knowing that at any moment the mass of bodies might collapse. Holding the lamp aloft, I was able to grasp the full extent of the horror around me.

Limbs were tangled together. There were a couple of uncovered faces, distorted by decay, teeth bared, the skin stretched. I didn't dare let my attention stay for too long on any one sight, lest it be burned into my memory for the rest of my life. There then came a sound, muffled, soft and echoing, as though from some dark recess of memory. It was my mobile phone. I panicked and realized I'd lost my bag in the fall. Listening carefully, I managed to fix the direction of the sound, and reaching forward, I grabbed one of the shoulder straps and hauled the bag toward me.

Retrieving the handset wasn't as difficult as I'd expected, though I nearly emptied the entire contents of the bag onto the pile below me before managing to answer it.

"Hello?"

"Hi, Ash, it's Gina. Look—"

"Gina, listen," I said, both amazed and relieved to hear

her voice. "I'm in some serious trouble here. There's bodies, loads of them. I think—"

"Ash? I can't hear—"

Oh God, I thought. *Great time for the signal to fail.*

"Gina!" I was shouting now, no longer concerned about keeping quiet. If Mather had been in the room above, he would surely have made his presence known by that point. "Gina, can you hear me?"

". . . sh . . . breaking . . . all ba . . . ater . . . kay?"

"Hello? If you can hear me, Gina, call the police. Get them over here right now! There's a psycho on this island!"

". . ." Just static.

"Gina?" But she was gone. I looked forlornly at the screen. The quality of the reception was now irrelevant. The battery was dead.

I felt hopeless and lost. I'd been given an opportunity to summon help, and had quite possibly wasted it. It could be a long time before people started to worry seriously about my absence. I prayed Gina had heard enough to raise the alarm.

Getting myself out of that stinking hole wasn't as difficult as I'd feared. I left the lamp where it was, knowing there were more above. In the flickering light I threw my bag over my shoulder and made my way carefully over the soft lumps of flesh and cloth until the doorway was right above me. Ensuring that Mr. Hopkins was a safe distance away, I put first one then the other foot on what looked like an arm. It started to give way, so I tried the back instead. This too started to move, but it stopped after a second or two, so I decided to trust it. I jumped up, reaching for the ledge with both hands. Despite my best efforts, my fingers failed to get a hold and my flailing body fell backward onto the unstable pile. My feet went into the gap between two limbs, and for a moment I thought I'd disappear into the heap. I found a more solid perch and tried again. This time I managed to grab hold of the ledge and, heaving my body up, slid first one knee then the other onto the floor of the theater. Looking back down into the pit, I saw a pair of glowing green dots. I lay on the floor and lowered my arm down as far as possible. Mr. Hopkins walked forward, tensed himself, shaking slightly, then leaped up and clung to my shirtsleeve. I winced as his claws punctured the skin beneath the cloth, then raised him up and lowered him to the basement floor. He made a strange gurgling sound in the back of his throat, then turned and ran off out of the room. I retrieved my camera, lit another lamp, and followed the cat out of the basement.

I didn't catch up with Mr. Hopkins until I was outside in the daylight once more. My eyes stung after being in the dark, and my head had started to ache. After the foul air below, the oxygen outside was like a fine wine for the lungs. I paced around, drawing in breath after grateful breath, until I remembered the vulnerability of my position. I scanned the path in front of me, then walked a little way down it before sitting on a patch of grass by the trees. My nerves were making my limbs shake. I had to calm myself down and get my thoughts straight before doing anything else.

Mather, it seemed, was a murderer. Unless there was someone else on the island. Either way, it seemed unlikely that he could have been unaware of the bodies. They were still decomposing, so he must have been around when they were dumped here, and could easily have had something to do with them. I was in serious trouble.

My breathing slowed and became regular. The oxygen seemed to be helping me think a little more clearly now. Bizarrely, I couldn't help but see the whole situation from a journalist's perspective. This was one hell of a story, definitely something for the national papers. The scoop of a lifetime. It was hard to get my head round everything, though. Why kill so many people? And why dump the bodies in that pit? The room above the pit was also a mystery, unless . . . Suddenly I remembered the peculiar color of the table and the floor. Was it blood? Had Mather been conducting experiments on people to satisfy some dark, twisted curiosity? It occurred to me that he might in fact have continued the experiments initiated by his old friend Soames. But how much of what he'd told me had been the truth? Was he really the innocent party in that whole sorry affair? Had Soames even existed? Was he bringing people to the island so that he could butcher them, remove their organs? It seemed insane then that he should tell me the story of Soames and the tramp. It was almost as though he'd been playing with me. Perhaps it was all an act to pull me in. How long would he have waited before drugging or killing me, and carrying me down into that basement to be a guinea pig for one of his morbid experiments? And the question about an accomplice remained. Luring all those people and killing them would be a huge endeavor to embark upon alone. Was there someone else on the island?

The victims now rotting in the basement must have been missed by family and friends. It made me think again of Gina and the aborted phone call. Had she heard anything? If not, how long before she realized something was wrong? Mum and Dad were visiting relatives in America, so they would be none the wiser. My sister, Carol, lived in Wales, and was rarely in to answer the phone. She wouldn't know if I was missing or not until Sunday, when I failed to make my weekly call. My friends would think nothing of me being out of contact with them for a few days. Unless Gina and the others at work knew something was up, I was screwed.

I pondered the question of how Mather had selected his victims. He struck me as the sort of man who would do things methodically. After all, he had plenty of time to plan in great detail. He must have seduced them all with the promise of seeing the Ganges Red. And once they were on the island, cut off from civilization by a good mile or two, they were his.

But why the mosquito? Why that creature in particular? And surely he could have drawn people to the island and killed them without them seeing even the faintest glimpse of it. Why had he gone to the trouble of showing me the insect and filling me in on the myth surrounding her? It seemed pointless. Whatever was really going on, it was anything but straightforward. Perhaps he had some grand scheme that required the presence of the Ganges Red. If Mather *had* been conducting his experiments on the island, maybe the mosquito was in some way involved. I couldn't quite see the connection, but I had a strong feeling that there was one.

I thought about getting to the mainland. My only concern was putting as much distance between myself and Mather as possible. And yet, I was fascinated. My curiosity couldn't leave the matter alone. I wanted to flee, but at the same time I wanted to uncover the truth. Every last bit of it. I guess that's what it means to be a journalist. I would be putting my head in the lion's mouth, but if I was to get to the bottom of this horror, I'd have to get Mather to spill the beans. At the very least I'd need my tape recorder, which, like a fool, I'd left in the living room. Mather's words, coupled with the mass grave in the basement of the research center, which I really ought to have photographed, would make for damning evidence indeed. But once more my mind was flooded with the danger of the situation. I decided not to push my luck. If I could get over to Tryst, I could find the police and tell them everything. Mather's secret would be exposed, and there was still a good chance that I would have the exclusive story. After all, who better than me to write it?

I stood and brushed myself down. There were now patches of damp on my trousers and shoes from contact

126

with the bodies in the pit, the mere sight of which made me retch. By my watch it was just after ten-thirty. Mather might already be out looking for me. I needed to move. The boathouse wasn't far away: if I didn't make too much noise, I could be out on the lake before he realized what was going on.

As I jogged along the path, my mind hovered over Mather's character. When I first arrived on the island he'd seemed so charming and welcoming. The way he talked, the subjects that interested him had made him seem like someone I, and no doubt a lot of people, could get along with. But all that solitude must have taken its toll on the man's mind. The charnel pit was proof of that. But why had he appeared so normal, so sane? Was he cleverer than he appeared? Was he a criminal genius? The fact that he could think rationally made him all the more frightening. If he'd been mad, my suspicions would have been aroused a lot earlier. And what of the Ganges Red? Was it really as lethal as Mather had made out? I'd seen a huge mosquito, but for all I knew it could have been a harmless freak of nature, or perhaps a clever trick, an illusion. As before, I was confused by the oddity of the plan. Why use such unusual bait?

I reached the gate and clambered over. I kept looking in the undergrowth around me. Mather might have been watching me when I'd left the clearing, might have guessed which direction I'd take.

Before long I came to the top of the slope that led down to the small beach and the boathouse. Without hesitation,

I ran down the slope to the small shed, kicking up clouds of sand as I went. In a blind panic I pulled at the door of the hut, trying to wrench it open.

"Mr. Reeves."

I froze. It was impossible to turn and face him. All I could do was stare at the warped wood of the door before me as he approached.

"What on earth are you up to? If you were that desperate to get home, you need only have said so. As a matter of fact, I was just coming to collect you."

"Sorry," I said, unsure of how to continue. "I . . . I don't know what came over me." I took my hands away from the wood and managed to turn and face him, offering what must have looked like a forced smile.

"It's all right. You are a long way from home, after all." Mather noticed the damp stains of death and dirt on my trousers but said nothing. He grinned, then looked up at the sky. "It seems to be getting colder, and I don't doubt there'll be more rain this afternoon. How about a nice cup of tea before we set off?"

"Um . . . yes . . ." I wanted to argue, to tell him I had to leave straightaway, but I could hardly speak. I was terrified.

We walked back up the slope and toward the clearing. My escape attempt had been thwarted. How much Mather suspected was unclear, but to be safe I had to assume he knew everything. The unpleasant wet patches on my trousers were enough to give me away. Maybe there would be some way of getting away from him, if I could only stay alive long enough.

The front door was open when we arrived back at the house. I could hear music, though I couldn't remember seeing any hi-fi equipment of any kind. I walked in ahead of Mather, trying not to look as if I expected to be attacked at any moment. I stopped and he led me into the living room, where he told me to make myself comfortable. To my surprise, on a table near the fireplace was a gramophone. I'd never seen one up close before, let alone heard one. It was a handsome device. The large, trumpet-like horn was light green in color, with a darker green trim, and resembled a huge flower. The box it stood on was a light brown, polished wood with a glass window in the front panel revealing the inner workings. I looked down at the record that was revolving on the turntable. It took a few seconds because it was moving, but I managed to read the title of the classical piece: *La Main du Diable* performed by Pandemonium.

The title was French. The music was unusual: there didn't seem to be any noticeable arrangement or structure. Pandemonium were certainly accomplished, but in some places it sounded like a free-for-all, an improvised battle with instruments as weapons. The record sleeve was fairly worn and, where the light from the window caught the dark areas, layers upon layers of fingerprints could be seen. It was clearly a popular record.

Mather excused himself and left the room. I reflected

that if he had been playing music, he couldn't have been too anxious about the situation, unless this revealed yet another freakish side to his character. But perhaps I wasn't in as much danger as I'd feared. Returning cautiously to the hall, I tried to listen above the music. Nothing. I couldn't stand still, so I moved down the hall and found Mather's door open.

He was drawing the panel back across the front of the alcove where the Ganges Red had been hidden away. He did it quite slowly, unlike before, as though he didn't want to make any noise. Something caused him to turn, and he jumped when he saw me standing by the door. He put a hand on his chest somewhat dramatically, then chuckled.

"Good Lord. You gave me quite a start."

"I'm sorry, I was just—"

"Forget about it." He looked back at the false wall, then walked toward me. "Now then, how about that tea?"

"Actually, I'm fine, I—"

"Well, let's go into the living room anyway." Although I'd startled him, Mather now seemed fairly calm, as though things were progressing as he had hoped. My unease grew. It was hard to know what to make of his behavior.

Back in the living room, Mather strolled over to the gramophone and lifted the needle from the record, which had finished playing.

"An interesting piece," I remarked, trying to sound calm.

"A masterpiece, as far as I am concerned. Pandemonium only produced a small number of works, but what works! The effect, the way they stimulate the mind, is just sublime. Inspired work." He picked up the record, balancing it carefully on the index finger of one hand, then slid it expertly into the sleeve. He walked over to one of the small floor cupboards and pushed the record inside.

"Now then, Mr. Reeves"—he gestured to a chair—"make yourself comfortable."

I put down the bag and camera and perched on the armchair. Mather took his usual seat, crossing his legs with an easy, comfortable manner. If he was brimming with malicious intent, he was hiding it well. "Did you see anything of interest on your long walk?"

I didn't like his use of the word "long." It implied that I'd been away for longer than expected.

"Not really. I saw a fair bit of the island. The other beach, the forest, the—"

"Research center?" The way he finished my sentence caught me by surprise and unsettled me. I'd already decided that it was pointless to lie about the place. Given how long I'd been away, it was unlikely that I'd missed it.

"Er, yes. Yes, I did. Didn't you say that there were no other buildings on the island?" There was a waver in my voice. I prayed it betrayed no nervousness.

"To be honest, it slipped my mind. I don't go to that side of the island, you see. I had a look around when I first came here, but there's nothing of any real interest there."

"I see."

Mather remained calm, and was almost convincing. But

he was probably used to dealing with the subject by now, and had planned his story, his excuses.

"It's no longer in use, of course," he said. "It was shut down years ago due to lack of funding."

"I see." Acrobats were performing in my stomach. *You liar,* I thought. *You've been near it, all right. And I know exactly what you've been doing in there. I'm going to make sure the rest of the world knows too.*

Mather cast me a meaningful look. It was as though in the mere seconds his eyes had been boring into mine, he had read my thoughts and understood my intent. "So, did you . . . take a look inside?"

"No." Damn. I said it far too quickly. Mather looked at me with one raised, enquiring eyebrow.

"No, I didn't," I said after a pause. "It didn't look too safe. I had a look around outside, though."

"Right." Mather glanced casually out of the window, a slight smile remaining on his face. "You know, thinking about it, you might actually find what's inside rather intriguing."

"Really?" I tried to appear surprised. "Why's that?"

"Well, apparently, before the center was closed down a lot of interesting work was done there."

Yes, and a lot more work's been done since it closed too!

". . . at all?"

"Sorry?" I'd been listening too much to my own thoughts to hear the question.

Mather smiled. He seemed amused by my behavior. "I asked if you were interested in marine life?"

"Oh. Well, not particularly. Although, I have written a few stories for the magazine about fish. Nothing really important, though."

"I see. Well, I think," he said, getting to his feet, "you would find the center quite fascinating. Why don't we take a quick walk over there now before we head back to the mainland? It'll only take a few minutes."

I looked up at him, a weak smile on my face, trying to think quickly. I could have said no. I could have said that I was eager to get back home, that I had a lot of work to do. But what then? Would he decide he had no other option but to murder me on the spot?

"Yes, OK," I said, almost without thinking. I had to say something, and I don't think I ultimately had the guts to say no. If Mather was indeed playing games with me, then I had to play along with him. My survival depended on it. "I suppose it can't hurt," I said, affecting another fake smile.

"Splendid. It shouldn't take long."

I wondered if he was actually enjoying himself. He walked off toward the kitchen while I desperately tried to think ahead. His plan must have been to either kill or incapacitate me, depending on what end he had in mind for me. If I was to gain the upper hand, I'd have to strike before we got to the building. But what could I do? Bash him over the head with a log? Push him into the lake? I didn't know if I had it in me to do either.

He came back into the room wearing a blue waterproof jacket. I stood up.

"Right," Mather said. "Shall we be off?" He clapped his hands and walked to the front door. I picked up my bag and camera and followed.

"Oh, just a second." I remembered the tape recorder and picked it up off the arm of the chair. When I rejoined Mather he was wearing an amused smile.

"Mustn't forget that," he said, stepping outside.

"No, we mustn't," I replied, following.

As I crossed the threshold I heard a strange voice.

Don't turn your back.

I thought it was a woman's voice, though it sounded distorted, like a really bad radio transmission. I looked at Mather, who was standing by the path. He was waiting patiently, and showed no signs of having heard the sound. He started to look at me quizzically, wondering, no doubt, why I was hesitating.

Do not turn your back on him!

This time the voice was louder and clearer than before, and it felt as if it were inside my head. But it didn't seem like a thought; it was as if someone—or something—was communicating with me. Mather looked as though he was about to do something, suspecting perhaps that I was up to no good. I preempted him.

"Sorry," I said, walking over. "I thought for a minute that it had started to rain." Thankfully, the sky overhead was now gray, reinforcing my story.

Mather looked up. "Mmm. Yes, we shall have to take care. Still, I don't think it's going to be as bad as yesterday." With that, he turned and trudged off along the path.

I hesitated briefly, waiting for another warning, but whoever or whatever had spoken to me was now silent. I followed Mather's footsteps into the trees, happy at least that *he* had his back to *me,* and not the other way round.

VIII: TREPIDATION

Mather seemed quite content to walk on ahead. Perhaps he saw no threat, even though he was giving me an opportunity to attack him. I lacked the courage to take drastic action right then, but what made it even harder was the fact that he seemed so infuriatingly sure of himself. I was convinced that he knew I'd been in the basement. So why was he so unafraid? Why wasn't he on his guard?

As we passed the second beach, I saw him cast a quick glance toward the boathouse. Maybe he did it on purpose, just to taunt me, maybe not—it was hard to tell, but I tried to keep myself calm and focused.

"I do hope you'll have enough material for your story," Mather remarked as we approached the gate. "I'd hate to think that I'd wasted your time. The Lady is an incredible specimen, but I sometimes wonder if I'm worthy of representing her, if you take my meaning."

"Oh, don't worry," I replied. "You've done an excellent job. I can't see how anyone could fail to be impressed."

"I hope you're right," he said, reaching round one side of the gate. I heard the sound of metal protesting, then a loud clang as Mather lifted a bolt of some kind and pushed the gate forward. Perhaps it had been the child in me, but when I'd approached the gate on my own, I'd instinctively climbed over it, not even considering the possibility that it might be unlocked. I couldn't help but feel foolish.

I walked past Mather, while he pushed the gate back into position behind me. I turned quickly, making sure I didn't have my back to him. He continued along the path with me in tow. Soon we were turning the corner and facing the research center.

We were almost at the porch when I noticed Mr. Hopkins lying on the roof of the building, licking one paw and blinking at us. Mather had also noticed the animal, but offered him only a brief scowl of disapproval. I was reminded of the Cheshire Cat from *Alice in Wonderland,* though Mr. Hopkins wasn't grinning. If anything, he looked uncomfortable. I sympathized. We entered the porch, Mather still leading the way, then went straight into the main hall.

"It's a rather unusual design for a research center." Mather walked into the middle of the room and stood gazing around. His attention lingered on the floor, as though he were looking for something, then, as I approached, he glanced up again. "When I had a look around some years ago, I expected to find a number of rooms, not just one. It's like an exhibition center. Though I can't imagine how they could have expected many visitors." My thoughts turned, inevitably, to the pile of bodies below us. "Still, it doesn't really matter now, does it?"

"No. I suppose not." I couldn't stop my eyes from

drifting to the basement door. It was wide open. If Mather made a habit of pulling it shut every time he had finished down there, he'd notice the difference. I tried to focus on him, worried that if he saw where my attention was wandering, his suspicions would be confirmed.

I made a show of strolling around the room and looking at the tanks and scientific equipment, always ensuring I knew exactly where Mather was. On more than one occasion I caught him looking down at the debris covering the floor. What the hell was he searching for? Something he'd lost? I heard the sound of something scraping on glass and, to my left, saw Mr. Hopkins pawing at a window. He seemed to register the fact that I'd noticed him and stopped scratching. At least someone was watching over me.

When I turned back to Mather, I caught him staring thoughtfully at the door to the basement. I switched my gaze to one of the damaged tanks so he wouldn't know that I'd seen him. In that moment all doubt left my mind. He knew what I'd been up to. He knew I'd discovered his foul secret. The question was, what was he going to do about it? Or, perhaps more importantly, what was *I* going to do about it? The latter was an easy question to answer. There was no way for me to get off the island without Mather's boat. Even if my phone hadn't been dead, I'd have had to get away from Mather to use it. He knew the island a lot better than I did. He could track me down in minutes. Again I prayed that Gina was doing something—anything—to send help. My sense of self-preservation was now all-consuming. The story no longer mattered: it could go to another journalist, or it could go to hell—I really didn't care.

My only concern now was to get myself off the island and back to civilization. In order to get hold of Mather's boat I would have to pry the lock off the boathouse door, which would be no easy task. To stand any chance of succeeding, Mather would have to be incapacitated. There was no escaping it: I would have to put him out of action. Running away was simply not an option. He'd have to be stunned and preferably tied up as well. I dreaded doing it, but I had no choice. I was roused from my thoughts by Mather's voice.

"Mr. Reeves! Come here, I want to show you something."

Oh God, I thought. *Here we go.* I walked over to him, my nerves jangling inside me. I felt as if I were going to explode. Mather didn't seem to find anything unusual in my behavior. Or if he did, he chose to ignore it.

"These stairs lead down to the basement."

"Oh, right."

"Mmm. I believe that all the really interesting research was conducted down there."

"Really?"

"Yes. Typical, I suppose, that all the best stuff is hidden away."

"Yes."

"Shall we take a look?"

"Well . . ."

"Wouldn't you like to see what they were hiding?"

"Er, where does that door opposite lead to?"

"Oh, that's just the staff room. Nothing of any interest there."

"Oh, I see."

"Are you all right, Mr. Reeves?"

"Mmm? Yes, I'm fine."

"You look a little pale."

"No, no, I'm fine."

"Well then, the basement awaits. Would you like to lead the way?"

"No." *God, no!*

"No?"

"Well, I mean, you've been here before. I might bump into something. It looks pretty dark down there."

"Oh my, yes. I'd forgotten, the lights are out of action. Don't worry, my flashlight is here somewhere. I left it behind last time."

Left it behind last time? You said you hadn't been here for years! Either Mather really was toying with me, or he was getting forgetful and revealing his lies without even knowing it. He gazed around the hall, scratching his head pointlessly.

"I must have left it in the store cupboard." I wished I'd searched the store cupboard earlier. The flashlight would have saved me from relying on my camera flash and the lamps for light.

Mather went through the opposite door, and I soon heard

him moving objects around, searching for the flashlight. My survival instinct took over. I looked quickly at the doors around me, trying to gauge which would be the best escape route. But Mather reappeared quicker than expected, a tiny Maglite in his hand. It was barely larger than a pen, and clearly insufficient for complete darkness. I was filled with dread. Going down into the gloom with Mather and only a pitiful beam of light for company was the most terrifying prospect I'd ever faced.

"It doesn't really matter," I assured him. "I'm sure it's very interesting, but—"

"Oh, it is. Don't worry, it may look treacherous, but I know my way." He grinned and winked. "Follow me." He entered the stairwell and took to the steps, holding the Maglite close to his right ear, pointing it down at an angle.

I hesitated. The basement was the last place on earth I wanted to go. Too late the thought occurred to me that I could have pushed him down those stone steps and maybe wedged the door to stop him from getting out. The fall might have broken his neck, or at the very least knocked him out for a while. But when at last I moved into the doorway, he was practically at the bottom. Now the opportunity was gone, and I had no way of knowing if I'd get another. I didn't want to kill Mather, but if it was the only way out, I would have to do it.

I went down the stairs, moving slowly, keeping him in view the whole time. When I reached the bottom, he made a show of brushing the light across all the walls of the room, exposing the unremarkable rubbish I'd seen already.

"Ah, er . . ." Something seemed to be missing. Mather was waving the light about, looking in vain for some object that wasn't where it should be.

"What's wrong?"

He shone the flashlight directly at me, blinding me and sending me into a sudden panic. In that split second I was unable to see anything but the brilliant light from the flashlight. He could have chosen that moment to do anything.

"Oh, sorry." He moved the light down, out of my eyes. "I'm sure there were an old oil lamp and some matches down here somewhere."

I had the distinct feeling that below the surface Mather was enjoying himself and relishing the control he exerted. But his unshakable confidence was a constant surprise. Why could he not see me as even a small threat? If I hadn't been so scared, I'd have felt insulted.

"Well, I suppose we'll have to manage," he said, looking a little put out. "I think this used to be a storeroom of some kind. Not much left, as you can see. I presume the staff members ransacked the place before they left. Took whatever they fancied. It's through there that all the top-secret work was done." He turned, shining the light into the doorway leading to what I now suspected was his operating theater. "Not much left to see, I'm afraid, but enough to get a good idea of what went on." He walked ahead, stooping slightly, as though expecting the doorway to be lower than it was.

Walking a few paces into the room, he stopped, pointed the light downward and started examining the floor. I moved up behind him, and by the light of the torch I could see that there were a number of deep, distinctive footprints leading to and from the lip of the doorway.

Oh shit, I thought. *Shit, shit, shit!*

He turned to me and smiled. "I tend to be a little more careful where I walk when I'm down here, Mr. Reeves."

I couldn't smile back. He shone the light toward the lip of the pit, then quickly back at me. Still he was calm, confident, in complete control. I stood there, momentarily paralyzed with fear. My tongue was fixed, my lips set. Even if I'd thought of something to do, I couldn't have done it just then. The terror was all-consuming.

Although the floor near the edge of the pit was relatively dry, we could both see clear signs of disturbance. I also noticed the odd smear of red on my boots and the legs of my trousers. *I've made it so easy for you, haven't I?*

"Sorry?"

I'd spoken the words completely involuntarily. But it seemed as if I had no will anymore. "Nothing."

"I see. It must have been quite a shock for you."

"What?"

"You fell, didn't you? Into the pit?"

Many seconds passed before I could answer. "Yes."

"Rather careless."

143

"Yes. I was surprised."

"I'll bet you were."

"No. I mean, I heard something moving behind me and I lost my balance."

"Moving? Who?" He sounded worried all of a sudden. What did he mean by "who?" There were only two of us on the island. Was he afraid that I hadn't come alone? Or did he think that some other visitor was on the island, moving about without his knowledge? Perhaps I could have benefited from lying to him at that point. Unfortunately, I didn't have the chance to find out. I only had enough energy, it seemed, for the truth.

"The cat . . . Mr. Hopkins."

"Oh." This calmed him somewhat. "That filthy creature. If only you'd done me the courtesy of wringing its scrawny little neck."

I couldn't think why he was so disgusted by the poor animal. Then, in a sudden movement, Mather pulled a small but cruelly sharp dagger from the waistband of his trousers. My stomach felt as if it were folding in on itself. I expected to be sick, but was thankfully spared the ordeal.

He held the strange, curving blade between us, but continued talking, as though it wasn't even there. "The number of times that foul pest has disturbed my work. It's as though he were put on this island to make my life a misery." Mather's eyes darted about the room, as if seeking the feline troublemaker. He took a few deep breaths, then seemed to calm down.

"Ah, well. He'll get his comeuppance soon enough. I'll see to that. Now then," he said, spotting a lamp on the floor. "Let us shed a little light on the subject." He lifted it up and placed it on the bloodstained table. Taking a box of matches from one pocket, he set about lighting the old lamp, gripping the Maglite between his teeth and pushing the dagger back under his belt. With some fiddling, he managed to strike a match and ignite the oil. When the flame had grown a little, he lifted it up and hung it from a hook in the ceiling.

"That's better." It was still fairly gloomy, but I could see now that the room was bigger than I'd previously perceived. In the wall to the right of the doorway above the pit was a recess housing a chest of drawers which may have contained tools and equipment. The floor was pretty much as I remembered it, although the sight of the many layers of congealed blood increased the queasiness in my stomach. "Well now," Mather continued. He switched off the flashlight and put it in his pocket. "I suppose you'd like to hear about what's been going on down here. No doubt your interest has been aroused." He carefully placed the dagger before him on the table.

"Well . . ."

"Hmm?"

"Well, if you really want to talk about it."

"If I want to? I would have thought that by now your curiosity would be so hungry it could eat a horse! Don't you want the full story? What I have to tell you could make you a very rich man indeed, if it were to be published.

Come on, young man, where are your journalistic instincts?"

I decided that if Mather wanted to procrastinate, that was fine with me. The more time he gave me, the more chance I had of figuring a way out of the living hell I was in.

"All right," I said.

I felt quite extraordinary—as if I was detaching myself from the horror of the situation and looking down on the two of us from the perspective of a third person. The looming shadows in the room, the pungency of death from the pit—both increased the sense of being caught within some grisly tale, fueled perhaps by fever, drugs or insanity. Mather leaned forward, his hands on the table, firm, controlled. I shrank back in fear. It was impossible not to wonder whether, in mere minutes, I might be nothing more than another lump in that grotesque heap below, one hand perhaps grasping above the tangle of limbs for help that would never come. It was the purest horror I'd ever faced.

"I was less than accurate in the story I told you earlier," Mather said.

"I'd gathered that," was my dry response.

He seemed amused by this. "You seem to be handling this better than I expected."

"Really?"

"Yes, I'm impressed."

I wished Mather would stop smiling like that. "Thank you," I said, with deliberate sarcasm.

"Hmm. Anyway, some elements of the story are true."

Here we go, I thought.

"Soames and I performed that first experiment pretty much as I described, except that I made no objection to it, either before or during."

"What about the homeless man?"

"Oh, he was real. My, how that man suffered. I actually toned down that part of the story. What actually happened was far more terrible."

I didn't want to listen, but neither did I want to risk upsetting Mather, not while his dagger was within easy reach.

"It almost ruined the experiment. A combination of alcohol, mutilation and sheer bewilderment drove that wretch to destroy himself. And I don't just mean suicide. I mean real destruction. He started by tearing his—"

"Please!" I couldn't take it. If he wanted to talk about his foul deeds, he could surely do it without certain details.

"I'm sorry, Mr. Reeves. I sometimes forget how desensitized I've become to all this. They're mere memories now. Nothing I've seen or done strikes me as being particularly gruesome anymore. To me it's a series of unfortunate incidents, punctuated by genuine scientific discoveries. And that is the important thing, after all. Soames and I made genuine progress in our studies. Not, I'm sure, that many people would see it that way. Society forgets all too quickly that some of the most important discoveries in history were made after and amid great pain and suffering."

I could feel the acid rising in my stomach. I didn't want to stand up anymore. I had to concentrate to keep myself together. If there was going to be even a slight chance of getting the better of Mather, I'd have to stay focused and alert.

"Soames knew, like I did, that we would have to get our hands dirty in order to make any real progress. He was always a little squeamish, but I was usually able to make him do what was necessary."

"So you were the one who initiated the experiments."

"Yes. I came up with the ideas. I was the one who had to do the convincing, the arm-twisting. It was hard work too. Soames had principles, you see. Rigid principles about conduct and so-called integrity. Ha." Mather laughed. "But he soon came round. I can be quite persuasive when I need to be," he said, stroking the hilt of the dagger.

"So what happened to him?"

"Soames . . . Soames lost his way. Some of my more extravagant ideas were just . . . too much for him."

"Extravagant?"

"Yes. Well, I suppose some people may have stronger words for it. There are very few things in life that shock me, Mr. Reeves. I must have a strong stomach. Or perhaps for me the most unpleasant sights and sounds are still part of the general wonder of nature. What sickens one person may delight another. It's all down to taste. And my tastes are admittedly . . . unique."

"Oh." I was loathing him more and more by the second.

"What I wanted, and what Soames always lacked the courage for, was to explore the unknown. To conduct the sort of experiments that had previously only been hinted at. Unwarranted organ extraction was just one of many ideas that came to me in my dreams."

"What else did you do?" I still hadn't formulated a plan of action to get myself out of the basement alive, but keeping Mather talking seemed like a good idea.

"You look quite unwell as it is, Mr. Reeves. Perhaps I shouldn't make things worse for you."

"No, really, I'm interested. As you say, all this would make a great story."

"Indeed. Although . . . perhaps this story should be kept between the two of us. . . ." He looked at me.

"Well, I can keep a secret. I wouldn't tell anyone if you didn't want me to."

"Oh, I would love to trust you, really. But I have more than my own well-being to think about. The Lady must be protected too. There is so much at stake, you see."

"But tell me," I said, trying to keep the conversation going, "besides the liver extraction, what else did you do?"

Mather chuckled at this. "Oh, we've barely scratched the surface yet. Can you imagine what else we extracted?"

"The heart?"

"No, no. What use would that be? Think more imaginatively."

"Lungs?"

"Mmm. Remarkable, if limited, results." He waited for me to make another suggestion.

This was easily the worst guessing game I'd ever played, but I had to keep him happy while I desperately sought a way out. "The kidneys?"

"Yes. Tried that twice, but both times the experiment was botched. Soames's fault entirely. He could be a clumsy oaf sometimes."

"Why did you choose him to help you? Weren't there more able students?"

"Oh, without a doubt. But finding ones who were willing as well as able—now that was a challenge. Luckily, I marked Soames out as a coconspirator from the moment I met him. The poor man thought I was just being friendly. I do regret deceiving him in that respect. He was greatly in need of companionship, so I befriended him, gained his trust and, in time, his obedience."

"Obedience?"

"Yes. I had to be in charge, in complete control, otherwise the work would have lacked focus. I was able to gradually shape Soames, change his way of thinking. Now he's little more than a drone, a slave—"

"You mean he's *here*?"

"I . . ." Mather was fazed for a moment. He knew he'd said something he shouldn't have. "My mistake. I've been alone for so long now. . . . Sometimes, having conversations with people who aren't really here is a way for me to stop myself from going a little strange. I often talk to Soames. It's silly, but necessary. Now then," he said, changing the subject, "what else do you think we removed?"

"Wouldn't it be quicker for me to guess what things you *didn't* remove?"

Mather didn't like that dry remark. His smile faltered slightly. "Come now, Mr. Reeves. That's hardly the attitude, is it?"

"No, I suppose not," I replied. "What about the brain?"

At this his eyes lit up and his broad smile returned. "Well, well, well. That was quite a jump, Mr. Reeves. From kidney to brain in one move. You tell me, though. Did we? Did we remove someone's brain?"

"No," I answered. "The results are too predictable."

"Bravo! Absolutely right."

The smell of decay, which up until then hadn't seemed as strong as before (probably obscured by the stronger smell of fear), was now reasserting itself. My stomach turned over again. I really needed to be out of there. But in that instant a question that had been buried in my mind since falling into the pit rose to the surface.

Why aren't there any flies around the bodies?

This caused me to break eye contact with Mather, to turn my attention to the pit. I listened for the sound of buzzing, for the sound of tiny, almost imperceptible wing movements. Nothing. I looked back at Mather. He'd noticed my distraction.

"Something wrong, Mr. Reeves?"

"No." I shook my head.

Mather reached out with his right hand and began softly stroking the snaking blade of the dagger. "Good. I'd hate to think I was boring—"

"Why aren't there any flies?" Maybe I said it to distract him, or maybe I genuinely sought the answer. Either way, the question was begging to be asked.

"I'm sorry?" He looked up, the smile fading a little.

"Flies. I haven't seen any." This was true and I think Mather picked up on the sincerity in my voice.

"I don't understand." He took his hand away from the dagger and walked round the table toward me. I sensed concern. I'd succeeded in throwing him off guard, so I continued.

"The bodies," I said, pointing to the pit. "They're in various stages of decomposition. There should be thousands of flies around them. What did you do, douse the bodies in insecticide?"

Mather looked confused now. He stepped closer to the pit, listening perhaps. "No, no, I didn't. Strange, it's never crossed my mind before."

But it has now. And it sounds as if it's bothering you.

"I suppose you're right. There should be . . ." He stepped even closer to the lip and carefully leaned forward, one hand on the doorway for support, straining to hear.

I knew this might be the only chance I was going to get, but I needed him to be just a little more off balance. "How often do you see insects on the island—besides the Lady, as you call her?" I asked, to keep him distracted.

"I hadn't really . . . That's very odd. I don't remember seeing any lately."

"Yes. Very strange." I was trying to think of how I

could continue to distract him, but it wasn't easy. Why *were* there no insects? If I knew, perhaps I could use it to further disrupt his concentration. As it turned out, though, I'd already done enough.

"My God," Mather uttered suddenly. "Of course!"

"What?"

"Oh, dear Lord. The dragonfly!"

"Dragonfly?"

"The Yemen dragonfly—it's him!"

"Who?"

"According to the myth his presence drives all lesser insects away. But I don't understand. If he's here, then she should have sensed him."

"She? You mean the Ganges Red?"

"Yes, the Lady. She would know—she must."

"The Yemen dragonfly?" The nightmare seemed to be taking an even more surreal turn. "What is that? What's so important about it?"

"The Yemen is the only creature capable of posing a threat to the Lady. She's in great danger while the Yemen is here. I must get back to her."

"The Yemen's more dangerous than her?"

"Oh, considerably more. She has told me often of the danger he poses. The thought of him upsets her greatly. She fears he intends to kill her. He is an incarnation of—" He was growing quite pale now.

"What?"

"He cannot be allowed to get to her!"

"Wait." I had to stall him. "It sounds as if there haven't

been any flies on the island for ages. Wouldn't that mean that the dragonfly has been here for some time?"

"Yes. He must have been waiting, biding his time. He could strike at any moment!" Mather turned again. He was eager to take care of business there and then so he could get back to the house. He eyed the dagger on the table. "Come, Mr. Reeves, there's no need for us to linger any longer."

Linger any longer? Oh, God, this is it. I'm going to die! I could see it all in his eyes.

His hand left the wall of the doorway and he began to move. Although still in the grip of terror, my instinct took over and I rushed forward, straight into him, stopping at the doorway and allowing the impetus to push him off the floor and down toward the mass of rotting flesh. His expression as he fell was almost comical. It was a look of stark surprise, of unfiltered panic. His hands flailed, but there was nothing for them to grab on to. I heard the dull thud of impact, the loud crack of a bone breaking, then silence. *Oh, my God,* I thought as I turned and fled. *I've broken his neck!*

IX: DEFAMATION

Taking Mather's advice, I didn't linger any longer. Tearing through the door, into the outer room and up the stone steps, I prayed that Mather's body had been swallowed up by the foul death mound of his own doing. When I reached the top of the stairs, I pulled the door to the stairwell shut, wedging it hard against the frame. I ran over and grabbed one of the stools lying on the floor, then jammed it under the door handle to make sure Mather couldn't turn it. If he managed to crawl out of that pit alive, I felt sure he'd never get through this door now. I sprinted down the length of the huge room, feet crunching on glass that had already been crushed into countless pieces, then burst into the reception area and out through the front door into the welcoming daylight.

I wanted to stop and hide myself in the trees, but instead kept on the path, aware that if Mather wasn't in fact dead, time was of the essence. When I reached the gate, I remembered to open it and went through. I wasn't far from the beach now, and I wondered how I was going to get the padlock off the door of the boathouse. Turning a bend, my head down, I was suddenly sure I was being watched. By the time I looked up it was too late, and I ran headlong into a tall figure blocking my way.

We both tumbled into the long grass by the side of the path. I was lucky not to have banged my head on the nearby tree stump. The stranger got to his feet quickly, brushing himself down. Holding out his hand, he helped me up. He was a lot taller than Mather and wore an old, worn shirt, trousers to match and shoes that had seen far better days. His hair was long and dirty and his eyes appeared bruised, which was perhaps the result of sleepless nights. His skin was the color of decay and he had the appearance of a man who was clinging to life for some unknown reason, as death had all but claimed him. In many ways he matched Mather's earlier description of Soames. But after all I'd seen, I wasn't quick to make assumptions.

"Help me! Please, you've got to—" I began, then stopped, sensing something wasn't right. Studying the expression on the man's face, I saw there was no surprise, no animation there, just a weary resignation, as though he'd been in this situation a dozen times.

"You must be Ashley Reeves," he said, looking anxiously past my shoulder toward the research center. "What have you done with him?"

"Are you Soames?" I wondered if I'd escaped one monster just to end up in the clutches of another.

"Yes."

"Oh, God!" I got to my feet and tried to run past him, but he grabbed my left arm and held on with surprising force.

"Wait! Whatever he's told you, you must trust me, we—"

"Look," I said, managing to jerk my arm free. "I'm getting off this island, so don't try and stop me."

"No, no. I won't. Is . . . is Mather dead?" I detected a note of hope in his enquiry.

"I don't know. I pushed him into the pit. He may have broken something, but—"

"Oh," he said, his smile fading. "Well, please, you must come with me if you want to get away." He turned and made to walk off into the trees.

I just stood where I was, looking up and down the path, wondering what the hell I was supposed to do. "Why should I trust you? How do I know you're not as twisted as he is?"

"No, no, no," he said, turning back to me. "Ignore what he's told you about me. He's—he's cleverer than you can possibly imagine. Now come on, before it's too . . . too late."

Soames's behavior was odd, but with only my instincts to rely on, I felt he was a far lesser evil than the one I'd left behind in the research center. I had to get away from the path, though, of that I was sure. I felt too exposed.

"You go where you want," I said. "I'm heading for the beach. Mather's boat is the only way off this island."

"No, no, no," Soames said again, shaking his head. "It isn't. It's no way off at all!"

"What?"

"You can get off the island, but not with the boat in

the boathouse. It's a joke of his. No bottom. Real boat's hidden away on another beach. I know how to get there, but Mather carries the ignition key with him. Now come on. You must come with me to my trailer, we can't linger on the path. He won't think of looking for you there, not to begin with. And there are things I must tell you."

"But—"

"Come on, there's no time to argue!"

"All right," I said. Knowing it could be a bad idea, I followed him into the trees. What he'd said about Mather and the boathouse sounded only too plausible.

We pushed through branches and leaves, putting distance between ourselves and the path. There were no discernible trails to follow, but Soames knew where he was going. The ground sloped upward after a while, and I slipped a couple of times, Soames stopping to wait but with obvious impatience. At length the ground leveled out and I saw what looked like a trailer, though the paint had long faded from its exterior, to be replaced by an angry coating of rust. Not a very welcoming sight, but for Soames it was home.

He climbed the small set of steps to the door in the trailer, opened it and ushered me in. He followed and closed the door behind him, indicating a stool for me by a curtained window. I sat, finding the seat somewhat lopsided. Soames drew the curtains across the other windows and sat on a more comfortable-looking chair by a small table littered with journals, papers and sticks of charcoal.

I could just make out that the surface of the table itself had been written on, like a school desk.

"Do you like the dark?" I wasn't too comfortable with Soames shutting out the daylight.

"It's a habit, you see. The only way I can get some privacy," he replied. "I can never tell if Mather is watching me at any time—this is the only way I can be alone."

"I see."

"I hope he's dead. Much better for us if he is." He looked me in the eye and nervously scratched the back of his right hand. "If he is still alive, he'll go to the boathouse first, and when he sees you're not there, he'll guess you've gone back to the house."

Now that we were able to rest, I could see how different Soames was from Mather. He had intelligence, but it was nothing like Mather's. My instinct told me that Soames wasn't the one I should be worried about. He carried none of the malice present in his colleague. He was too frail to be any kind of threat. I still kept my wits about me, but now listened more closely to what he said, realizing he might indeed be trying to help me.

"And what will he do when he realizes I'm not there?" I asked him.

"He'll search the whole island! Oh, yes. But he might not suspect that I've helped you at first."

"You will help me, then?" I asked, relieved. "Please, I've got to get away from here. We both have."

"Yes, I'll help you—but I don't care what happens to

me now. As long as he is finished. . . ." His eyes met mine.

"How many people have died here?"

"You saw the bodies in the pit?"

"Yes."

"That's not even half."

"There are more?"

"Mather—he used to just weight the bodies and dump them in the lake. That was until I convinced him that sooner or later they'd be found by fishermen—or tourists."

"How many, though?"

"You wouldn't believe it, Ashley."

"How do you know my name?"

"It was me who found you."

"Found me?"

"Yes. In *Missing Link.* That's how we bring people here. When Mather needed bodies for his experiments, he figured he could use the mosquito to lure people. He paid Derringher to—"

"Derringher?"

"The harbormaster."

"Oh, yes."

"He paid him to bring magazines and papers from the newsagent's in town twice a month. I would go through them and select people who might have an interest in the Ganges Red. Scientists, entomologists . . . journalists." He looked at me, then turned away. Pulling a curtain aside carefully, he peered out. "We would send out a letter to get their interest and just wait for them to show up. Some came, some didn't. We've had lots of visitors," he said, with a distant, regretful look in his eyes. "I never thought we'd get away with it for so long."

"But these people must be missed. What do you do when friends and relatives come looking for them?"

"Mather says that scientific magazines like yours aren't written by people who have much of a social life. They're loners mostly. And in his letters he always tells people not to mention where they're going. They think it's because the story is secret, but it's so they can't be traced here."

"But you're still taking a big risk."

"Yes, but that's where Derringher comes in. As well as getting us the magazines and stuff, he also puts people off the scent. If people start snooping around, he just tells them he's never seen anyone. They believe him."

"Mather pays Derringher to do that too?"

"Yes. He pays him well, I think."

"But what about the train station? What if someone there remembered seeing someone?"

"Tryst is small, but it does get a large number of visitors, even in the colder months. We get a lot of tourists and hikers. I doubt the guards at the train station would remember individuals."

I was growing colder and colder the more I learned of their foul scheme. Mather, it seemed, had thought of everything, and, judging by the number of bodies on or around the island, escape wasn't often an option.

"Look, we should both be getting off this bloody island in case Mather does manage to get out of that pit."

"First you must hear this. You must tell this story when you get back—I'll . . . I'll never . . . Just listen, please. It's important. Mather is only part of the danger you're in."

Despite the tense situation, my curiosity was getting the better of me. "Mather told me a story about his days as a medical student. He wanted me to believe that it was you who had done all those horrible things."

"Of course he did! It's all part of the trap, to make you feel sorry for him." There was something about Soames's manner, his urgency, that I believed.

"So what really happened?"

"Mather was the one who came up with the idea. He made me help him. Said he'd ruin my chances of graduating if I didn't help—"

"He was using you."

"Mmm. He must have had the idea for a long time, and wanted to get me to like him before he told me about it all . . ."

"He's a real piece of work," I said, shaking my head.

"But he's—he's the cleverest man I ever met," Soames said, with deep melancholy. "And the only real friend—"

"Friend?"

"Yes. He was the only one who ever listened to me, and I was honored to be associated with him."

"You don't really respect him, do you?"

"Of course!" He looked me in the eye with a shocked expression, as though I'd said something ridiculous. "He's sick, but he's . . . he's a genius!"

162

"A genius? How can you say that? He's a monster."

"What he's done over the years . . . the experiments . . . they're appalling . . . horrific. I never imagined a human being could do things like that to another. But I can't help but be in awe of his mind. He can do it all, over and over again . . . and his mind stays firm. Me, however—I didn't think I'd be helping him with his work for so long . . . I'm not sure I know who I am anymore. My mind is . . . different."

"I can't believe you stayed here all this time. You have to stop being a part of what's going on here."

"I haven't helped him for a long time now. There came a point when I no longer wanted to. He kept threatening to set that monster on me, and the threat worked for a while, but soon not even that could make me help him do those things. In a way I think he was pleased to have the bodies to himself for a change. Now I just find the names for him. But even that has to end. I want to finish him and his work. I won't pretend I'm any less guilty than he is. And I'm not helping you out of the goodness of my heart, I'm doing it because . . . it ends here."

"Forget about stopping him. Survival is more important. While he's down in that pit we can get off—"

"No, no, no. It's not as easy as that. You've seen the Ganges Red?"

"Yes."

"Without that creature, we wouldn't be here right now. If the mosquito had never found Mather, he would never have come here."

"But he told me he found the Ganges Red *after* coming here."

"More lies."

"Did he lie about everything?"

"No, not everything. It's all part of the game to him. The mosquito, for instance. I'll bet that whatever he told you about her is true. No legend, no myth, as ridiculous as it sounds. And *she* found Mather, not the other way round. She found him, and made him her slave."

"What?"

"You see, the Ganges Red isn't the one that's trapped . . . we are." Soames looked down at the floor. He seemed swathed in hopelessness.

"But it's just an insect, surely?"

"I wish." He looked up and shook his head. Suddenly we heard a branch snapping outside. A chill went through me. Had Mather escaped the research center? Surely not.

Soames reached over carefully and parted the curtains a little. He looked this way and that, then breathed a deep sigh of relief. "It's OK," he said. "It's just Mr. Hopkins."

"So . . ." I tried to regain my composure, but my heart was still beating twice as fast as it should. "How did you get involved with Mather's experiments in the first place?"

"I had a hard time at medical school and Mather used to stand up for me. When he asked me to help him with his work I thought he genuinely wanted to do some good, to benefit mankind. And I felt privileged." Soames sat back again. "Of course, in time I realized he was a psychopath."

"It was only when I found the pit and the bodies that

I realized there was something seriously wrong with him," I said. "He disguises it so well. What did you mean before, when you said the mosquito wasn't just an insect?"

"I can't begin to understand everything. All I know is what I've seen and heard." Soames rubbed his brow. "For some reason that creature deliberately chose Mather. She chose him because he was capable of doing what had to be done. I think she was somehow aware of his experiments, and decided she could use him."

"Use him? What do you mean? It's an insect!"

"She's not, though. What you see is just a shell, just like our bodies are shells. It's what's inside that's important. She wants blood, just like other mosquitoes. She satisfies her thirst with the victims Mather provides—but what she really wants is something else." Soames wrung his hands. He looked to me like a man confined to a prison cell. Mather must have really messed with his mind.

"An insect has no intelligence."

"Oh, but this one does," he insisted. He was smiling now, though there was no humor there, merely dread.

I decided for the moment not to argue with him about the mosquito. With the little time that I had, I wanted to get as much solid information as possible. "So, why come to this island? Was it because there was less chance of discovery?"

"Yes, I think so. In the city Mather knew that he would be caught sooner or later."

"So, how exactly did he find the mosquito? He told me a friend of his in Africa brought it to him."

"I'm still not entirely sure how it happened, but I can tell you what I remember. It would help if you knew a little more about the danger you're in."

"All right. But please, make it quick. We—"

"I know, I know." Soames tried to relax. In the shadows of the caravan, he was like some bleak specter, unsure which side of death he belonged to. I was desperate to get away but I couldn't help but be fascinated by the story that was unfolding.

X: ABSOLUTION

"There was something terrible in Mather's eyes on some occasions. I kept telling myself in the early days that it was my imagination, but I later realized there was something seriously wrong with him. The atrocities he committed— they couldn't all be for the sake of science."

Soames got to his feet and started pacing about the room.

"The night the Ganges Red entered our lives is one I'll never forget," he continued. "Mather had just finished an operation on a man he'd picked up outside a train station. He'd made long incisions into the man's wrists and severed all the tendons, before swapping them over and stitching them up. He wanted the man to think he was moving one finger, when he was really moving another. It was so pointless but I . . . Maybe it was the drinking, the drugs. I used to do them both. I never saw what happened to the ones who survived the experiments. He must have killed them afterward, otherwise they would have . . . Perhaps that's why he found it so easy to control me, because I was so high most of the time. Anyway, on this particular night we were waiting for the subject to wake up, when there was a sound at the door. It was a very light tapping. . . ." Soames chuckled. "On some occasions Mather and I thought the same thing, because he said the exact words that were in my head. '. . . *Suddenly there came a tapping, as of some one gently rapping, rapping at my chamber door.*'

"It's from Edgar Allan Poe's 'The Raven,' and hearing the words out loud made me uneasy. I went to the door and opened it. I've never felt so scared, so cold, as I did standing on that threshold and facing that monstrosity for the first time. It seemed to glow bright red. And the humming noise it made was like a horrible music. It hovered in front of me, then reared up, as if it was going to fly at my head. I covered my face with my hands, but it flew right past my ear, toward Mather.

"I turned round, expecting to see Mather fighting off the thing. But it had landed on the bust of Florence Nightingale that had belonged to Mather's late aunt. It looked as if it was watching Mather. Studying him.

"I closed the door and went over to the table. The patient's foot began twitching and I knew that he'd soon regain consciousness. Mather remained locked in the mosquito's gaze. He smiled, I think. I'd never seen an insect so big. Mather went over to the bust and stood there staring at the thing. He recited another line from the poem: '*Tell me what thy lordly name is on the Night's Plutonian shore!*'

"Its wings flapped faster; then it made this strange whining sound that cut straight through my head. The pain was terrible. I had the feeling that the creature was trying to block my thoughts, to stop me from hearing something. I went over to the other side of the room to try and clear my head. Mather was rubbing his forehead too, but he didn't seem to be in as much pain as I was. His mouth was wide open. So were his eyes. The insect was doing something to him. Something strange.

"On the table, the man's left arm twitched, and he let out a groan. *Oh, God,* I thought. *He's waking up.* I walked round to his head. His eyelids started to flicker. I turned to Mather for guidance, but he was still looking at the mosquito.

" 'For God's sake!' I shouted at him. 'Get over here! He's regaining consciousness.'

"Mather turned to me, smiling. 'Is he? That is convenient,' he said.

" 'Convenient? What are you talking about? He needs more anesthetic.'

" 'No!' Mather walked over to me and grabbed my wrist. 'Don't waste any more. He won't be needing it.'

" 'What?'

" 'You'll see.' He released my arm and looked back at the insect, nodding his head. 'Please,' he said to it. 'Be my guest.'

"I stared at Mather, wondering what madness had overcome him. Just then the mosquito rose into the air and flew straight over to the patient's neck.

" 'What's it doing? Why is—?' I guessed too late what was going to happen. It stuck its feeding tube into the poor man's jugular vein.

"I stepped backward in shock. If the size of the thing wasn't terrifying enough, the way it sucked up the victim's blood certainly was. Its body grew until it was more than double its original size. I tugged on Mather's shirt-sleeve.

" 'We should get out of here and call someone,' I said. 'Someone who deals with things like this.'

"The mosquito continued feeding until its body was bloated with blood. It removed its tube, fluttered its wings, then just sat there quietly.

" 'What a truly incredible sight,' Mather said.

" 'What the hell is it?'

" 'It's something very special, I know that much. Very special indeed.'

" 'Special? Good God, don't you think we—?' I broke off when I saw what was happening to the patient's throat.

"Mather had noticed it too. 'Good Lord,' he said under his breath. The insect flew off the patient and landed back on the bust.

"What had, a few moments before, been nothing more than a puncture wound was now a widening hole. Steam was rising from it, along with the dreadful stench of rotting flesh. The patient was now wide awake, and throwing his arms about in agony. And then . . . then he started screaming.

"The mosquito's saliva had eaten through the left half of the man's neck. It was so horrible. I tried to end his suffering by injecting a lethal dose of morphine, but Mather stopped me and held me back. I had to watch as that poor man died. Mather's mind had gone through some kind of change that night. He'd done terrible things before then, but from that night they just got worse. I was about to say I'd go to the police, but before I could speak the mosquito flew up and landed on the tabletop in front of me.

" 'I know what you are going to say,' Mather whispered in my ear. 'And so does she.'

" 'What are you talking about?' I struggled, trying to break away from Mather, but his hold was too strong and he just laughed. Eventually he decided to let me go. I staggered away from the table, stepping into the pool of blood on the floor.

" 'It seems the Lady here has been looking for a fellow like myself for some time.' He smiled and held out his hand. The mosquito flew up and landed on his palm.

" 'What are you doing? Get away from that thing—it'll kill you!' I took another step backward toward the door.

"Mather started laughing. It was an awful sound. 'She means me no harm, Soames. Salvation comes in many guises.'

" 'Salvation? What are you talking about?'

" 'I'm not entirely sure yet. But I will know in time.' He looked down at the mosquito with what looked like adoration. 'I believe she has much to teach me.' He chuckled again. 'Now be a good fellow and don't upset her. You wouldn't want to go the same way as this poor chap, now would you?'

" 'My God, look at this mess, Mather! That thing's dangerous! We need to tell someone.'

" 'What are you talking about? Tell someone?' He came closer to me, staring me in the eye. 'What do you think will happen if you divulge the details of our experiments to the police? Hmm? They'll lock us both up and throw away the key. You know that. That's, of course, if *she* doesn't get you first.'

"The idea of being that creature's next victim was more than I could bear. It seemed to have some control over Mather. It showed no sign of hostility toward him. In fact, after that night the pair were inseparable. I continued to help him with his experiments, even when it became obvious that there was no longer even a shred of scientific curiosity left in him. He was getting pleasure from mutilating those poor people, but he would always defend himself whenever I questioned his methods. He would tell me that it was the only way to learn more about the human body, and about the connection between body and mind.

"Soon after that awful night Mather announced that he was moving away from London to an island he had bought. I asked him how he'd managed to buy an entire island, and he told me some story about an inheritance. He didn't convince me, despite his continued assurances. I tried to break away from him and begged him to leave me behind, but he wouldn't listen. He didn't trust me. Perhaps he was right not to.

"Suddenly one day he invited me to his house on a matter of great urgency. When I arrived I asked him if something terrible had happened. He replied that if anything, it was good news. The Ganges Red was with him, and seemed to be just as excited. He said he had to go to the island for a day or so to make sure everything was ready for the move. I must have gone quite pale when he informed me that the Lady would be staying behind to keep an eye on me. I insisted that there was no need, that I wouldn't cause any trouble, but he didn't even pretend to be listening.

"So he went away that night, leaving me with the mosquito, which seemed to take great pleasure in guarding me. I was able to move about the house freely, but other than that I was a prisoner. I found it odd that Mather was able to leave the insect. Until then they hadn't been out of each other's company. The second night following his departure, he returned. He didn't say much about how the trip had gone, just that everything was as it should be, and that we could move the following week. I didn't bother repeating my desire to stay behind. It wouldn't have done any good.

"We've been here many years now. I think I've lost track of time. The house was already here when we arrived— I don't know what happened to the previous owner. This trailer was also here, and Mather told me to make it my home. He would let me know when he wanted my help. He brings me food once a week. It isn't much, but it's enough to survive on. I feel like an animal in many ways. A caged animal, free only to serve its master. But what else can I do? I can't go back to normal society now. Not after all I've seen and done. And I know that Mather would release the mosquito to hunt me down and kill me. No, there's no way I can escape."

Soames was a tired man. Tired from a great many things. He pulled the curtain aside and peeped out again.

"He still brings you food? Even though you don't help him with the experiments anymore?"

"Yes—I don't think he can completely abandon me. Nor, I think, does he want to kill me—unless he has to. We've been through a lot together. As funny as it sounds, I think he does see me as a friend. Even if he doesn't realize it himself."

"Haven't you ever tried to escape?"

"Where would I go? What would I do? I'm bound to Mather, to this island, to the horrors I've seen. I can't leave. I wouldn't know how to survive. And then there's her—"

"*Her?*"

"Mather has a book. It's called *Her Story*. In it is a—"

"Wait. I read that. Well, part of it. Mather pointed me to a chapter called 'The Legend of Nhan'—"

" 'Diep.' "

"Yes, that's it."

"You read the story?"

"Some of it. Mather filled me in on a little more this morning. He told me something about her leaving her husband for a merchant."

"Yes, without that merchant things might have been different."

"Is the story important in some way?"

"It explains, perhaps, everything."

"But it's another myth, isn't it? Just like the Ganges Red being able to . . . enter men's minds."

"I think there's some truth in all of it. Please let me tell you the rest of the story. It may help you."

"OK . . ."

"I'll be quick, I promise. Now let me see . . . the merchant's ship . . . Oh, yes, Nhan Diep was treated like a queen. She no longer had to work, except at keeping herself pretty for her new husband."

I met Soames's tortured eyes, feeling that perhaps this conversation was as much for his benefit as for mine. He hadn't spoken to anyone but Mather for a long time. It must have been a great relief to be around someone else.

"Ngoc Tam spent many days searching for his wife," he continued, "whom he believed had been abducted. He was leaving a large port one day with food for his ongoing journey when he caught sight of her, sunning herself on the deck of the large vessel she now called home. He dropped the supplies he was carrying and stared at her, barely able to believe what he was seeing. Just then the merchant came out of his cabin, kissed Diep tenderly on the cheek and lay down beside her. Tam was furious. He stormed onto the merchant's ship, knocking two startled guards into the water in his rage. He demanded to know what was going on, and listened in astonishment as Diep said she had chosen to be with the merchant, who had promised to give her anything she wished. Tam was silent for some time, then nodded and resigned himself to the fact that the lady was no longer his. But before he left he demanded that she give back the three drops of blood he had shed to restore her life. Diep laughed and shrugged her shoulders. She took a fruit knife from a bowl nearby and cut the tip of her right forefinger—"

"She gave him his blood back?"

"Well, she believed he'd gone mad and just wanted to humor him, hoping he would leave her alone. Anyway, when Tam caught the blood in the palm of his hand, a transformation occurred. Diep rose from the cushions where she'd been lounging and began to shrink in size, her body twisting and folding in on itself. Tam and the merchant backed away, horrified by what they were seeing. In seconds Diep was the size of a bird. But unlike a bird she had a long needle extending downward from her head. A needle designed for only one thing."

"Blood."

"Exactly. But not just any blood. She wanted Tam's blood. It was the only way she could become a woman again. She flew at him but he swatted her away, stunning her. By the time she was able to take to the air once more, Tam had gone. But Diep couldn't find her way home. She had to search endlessly, desperately for her husband. . . ."

Soames pursed his lips, clasped his hands and stared down at his feet. Then he chuckled. "Despite everything, it's a wonderful story," he said.

"Yes. But again, what bearing does it have on our situation?"

"I believe the story explains the Ganges Red."

"What? You believe . . . the Ganges Red is . . . Nhan Diep?"

"Yes."

"You're joking. Why?"

"Why not? I've heard stranger things."

"I haven't."

"If you believe the stories about the Ganges Red, witness the strange effect she has on Mather and her lust for blood despite the fact that she can't reproduce, then—"

"Wow." I laughed. "That's a pretty big leap. Sure, the mosquito is incredible, but it's a freak of nature, that's all. There's no evidence to suggest it has any connection to the myth. I mean, have you ever experienced any strange phenomena when near her?"

"Not directly. But she communicates with Mather, of that I'm sure."

"Oh, he's imagining it all. . . . Either that, or he's just playing with you."

"No, no. Before she arrived, Mather was behaving normally—well, apart from the experiments."

"All right," I said. "If I take a huge leap of imagination and believe this is true, then what exactly is Nhan Diep doing here? What's her plan?"

"I believe she's making Mather help her. He and I draw people to this island, and she feeds on them, hoping that one day she'll find—"

"The blood of her husband? That's crazy!"

"Yes, well, Mather is convinced of it. I know he is. And whether it's true or not, his belief in it is dangerous enough."

I looked at Soames's drawn face, his sharp, pale features. He was a prisoner, and he looked the part.

"OK," I said. "Isn't it about time we were getting the hell out of here?"

"I told you, I'm not going anywhere."

"But—"

"I can't leave."

"Why?"

"Haven't you been listening? I can't go back to civilization now. And besides—I think she would know if I tried to leave. Even if I could get off the island alive, she might track me down. And she'd make me sorry. You have a chance, though. You haven't been exposed to her for long enough—"

"In that case I'll send help as soon as I get to the mainland." I stood up. "In the basement Mather said something about a dragonfly. He seemed pretty worked up about it. Does this mean anything to you?"

"I don't remember him saying anything about a dragonfly. Unless it's . . ." Soames's brow furrowed as he thought something over.

"He sees it as a threat," I said. "I think he called it the Yemen or something."

"The Yemen! Yes. So the Yemen is a dragonfly . . .

Now it all makes sense. Dragonflies prey on mosquitoes. He must have come for her."

"Who is he?"

"You remember the genie in the Nhan Diep story?"

"Yes." *Not that again,* I thought.

"One of the forms he took was that of a dragonfly. And he's supposedly immortal—so maybe it really is true. Maybe he's come for her, to stop her. That would explain why all the flies have gone."

"You noticed that too?"

"Yes. He must have been here for some time, watching her, making sure he had definitely found her. He would be able to banish the other insects so that he wouldn't be distracted in his observation. The Yemen dragonfly must be a modern name, like Ganges Red. He must have been hunting her for a long time. All the more reason for you to get away from here as soon as possible. It's the sort of confrontation you'll not want to be in the middle of."

I thought the man must be delusional. He honestly believed in this whole myth as much as Mather did. I made a final attempt to persuade him to leave the island with me.

"Ashley, the last thing I deserve from anybody is sympathy. I gave up that right a long time ago. I'm just as much a monster as Mather or the Lady."

"So you intend to die here?"

"My fate is linked with Mather's. Always has been."

I thought this over for a while. Despite all he'd done,

it was impossible not to feel sorry for Soames. He'd defied Mather when things had gone too far, and had then been forced, against his will, to continue helping him.

"So, how do I get off the island if I can't use Mather's boat?"

"I'll show you," he said, getting to his feet and carefully opening the door of the trailer.

We both looked cautiously around for any sign of Mather, listening for telltale rustling or the snapping of branches. When he was happy that we were alone, Soames looked back at me and nodded that it was OK to proceed. It was approaching one o'clock. I wanted desperately to be on my way home, putting as much distance between myself and the island as possible.

"Come on," Soames said.

I had no idea where he was taking me. My instinct told me we were heading in the direction of the house, but if that were so, then we should have come upon the path at some point. After about five minutes Soames stopped at the top of a small rise. He waited for me to catch up.

"It's down there. At the bottom of the hill." We started down the incline.

"But there's nothing down there," I said.

Soames didn't reply, so I just carried on after him, sliding down the hill in bursts so I wouldn't fall and roll down.

When I reached the bottom, Soames was standing in the middle of a small clearing, facing me. I stood beside him, a questioning look on my face. He looked down at the ground by our feet. I followed his gaze and at first could see nothing of any interest amid the soil, leaves and twigs. Then I saw it.

It was well camouflaged—a short length of thick, old rope, poking out of the ground no more than an inch. Both ends appeared to be beneath the surface of autumnal detritus, presumably attached to something.

"Using this tunnel to the mainland should be safer than using Mather's boat."

Soames knelt down and grabbed hold of the rope with both hands. Slowly, he straightened his body, pushing with his legs and pulling on the rope with all his strength. As I bent down to watch, the rope lifted, and a large patch of square ground came up with it. It was a wooden hatch. All of a sudden there was a strange, loud noise and Soames let go of the rope handle. I looked up to see him stumbling backward, raising his hands to his forehead, which was now bleeding profusely.

He slipped and fell onto his back, banging his head hard on the ground. Then he lay very still. I knew what had happened even before I could confirm it. Turning very slowly, I saw the desperate figure holding a spade above his head, ready to strike a second time. The look in his eyes wasn't one of anger or revenge; it was pure murder. I had less than a second to prepare before the hard, cold blade of Mather's shovel connected with my face as well.

XI: CONGREGATION

I can't really explain how nauseous I felt on regaining consciousness. It was perhaps like waking from a car crash with a bad hangover. Mather had moved me from the spot where I'd fallen, but exactly where he'd left me remained a mystery until I was able to focus properly. It looked different, but I was definitely in the clearing by the house, and the sun was setting. Another sharp pain lanced across my head, making me groan. I couldn't hear much due to the awful ringing in my ears. The need to vomit became urgent, but standing up wasn't an option: Mather had tied me to a tree with a length of tough rope. He'd arranged me so that I was facing the clearing, with the house to my left. I tried to twist my way round the tree, in the hope of loosening the rope, but it was a wasted effort.

Mather must have pulled my hands together at the back of the tree, then bound them. He'd then tied rope around my waist, securing that to the tree as well. He was clearly taking no chances. I pulled at my bonds a few times, in the hope of working them loose. No such luck. I'd have to wait until my head cleared and my strength returned. So I just sat there, eyes closed, helpless, hoping that Mather wouldn't return for a long, long time.

I must have passed out again, because when my eyes opened next, night had consumed the island. A full moon peeked from between dark clouds to bathe the area in a pale blue light. Occasionally I heard a bird or some other creature move among the branches overhead, or dart through the leaves on the forest floor, but otherwise it was quiet. I felt pitifully alone, and more vulnerable than I'd ever been.

It was some time later—I've no idea how long—when a pair of luminous green dots appeared by the side of one of the trees on the opposite side of the clearing. At first I panicked, wondering what strange feral creature had taken an interest in me. Then I realized the eyes must belong to a cat, and as far as I knew there was only one in the vicinity.

He sat there watching me, perhaps wondering what to make of my predicament. After a short while he padded over. He looked a lot better in the dark. He even seemed to move with a little more grace and dignity. Perhaps the night brought out the best in him.

He reached my feet, then settled down on his stomach between my legs. He was like a tiny sphinx as he stared up at me, head tilted curiously to one side.

"Things aren't looking good," I said, my voice sounding foreign to me. It was hoarse, weak, as though I'd been shouting for hours. "My head feels as if it's going to burst."

The cat sneezed, made a contented gurgling sound,

then started to purr. At least one of us was comfortable. Mr. Hopkins's left ear flicked as though in reaction to something. It was a raindrop. He got up, turned and took off into the trees, seeking better cover.

As the rain began to fall in earnest, I gazed resentfully upward, wondering what reason the Almighty could possibly have to dislike me. Strangely, the rain seemed to alleviate some of the pain in my head and the aching in my wrists. I closed my eyes, expecting to black out again.

"Who knows?"

It was almost a whisper, and I couldn't be sure from which direction it had come. I opened my eyes and saw no one. The rain had stopped, but it was still dark and the moon had emerged again from behind the clouds. Drops of water were falling from my hair and eyebrows. My clothes felt sodden and the aching in my bound wrists was worse than ever.

"Who knows?"

I winced. Mather had repeated the question louder than before, and directly into my left ear. Pain exploded inside my head. He moved in front of me and shone a flashlight into my eyes.

"Answer me. Who knows you're here?"

"I don't know. . . ."

"Of course you do."

"Well, my editor . . . some of the others in the office."

"Family, friends?" He was agitated.

"Yes, a few of them," I lied.

He came right up to me and poked the wicked, curved

dagger beneath my chin. I swallowed, then concentrated on not moving my head.

"The letter instructed you to tell no one. Now—the truth!"

"Well, my editor knows . . . and Gina."

"Who?"

"She's the photographer at the magazine. I think I mentioned to her—"

"You'd better not be messing around with me, Mr. Reeves." Mather was whispering again. "I can't begin to illustrate the consequences for you if you are." After a few tense seconds he removed the dagger and pushed it back in his belt.

"Where's . . . ?" My throat felt terribly dry. "Where's Soames?"

"Soames is dead. Very dead."

"What do you mean, *very dead*? What did you do?" The oppressive need to close my eyes and sleep again was becoming unbearable, but I wanted to hear Mather's response.

"Do you know what the optic nerve is?"

"Something to do with the eye," I mumbled.

"That's right. It's the stalk that connects the eye to the brain."

"So?"

"Soames once joked that he'd love to see what his insides looked like. Well, now he has! It's amazing how far the optic nerve can stretch." He grinned.

I felt sick. "You've no idea how insane you are, do you?

185

I dread to think what the police are going to make of what's in that pit."

"Not a lot," he replied, smiling. "I'll see to that. You know, not all the bodies are in there."

"I know. You dumped some in the lake."

"That's right."

"Soames also said that you inherited the house. But you told me earlier that you bought it from an old guy."

"Yes, I did say that, didn't I?" Mather chuckled, scratching his chin absently and staring up at the night sky. "My, my—you poor man. I'll bet you don't know what to believe."

"Well, let's just say I'm taking everything you say with a grain of salt from now on." I'm not sure what kept me talking. Perhaps I was still trying to delay the inevitable.

"As a matter of fact, I did take the house from an old gentleman—Mr. West. But I didn't exactly buy it from him."

"And did he end up on the operating table too?" I gave Mather a nasty look, but it didn't seem to bother him.

"No—the theater wasn't set up then. Besides, I wanted to deal with the problem quickly and get back home. I didn't like the idea of Soames being alone with the Lady." For a foolish moment I actually believed Mather was showing concern for his late accomplice. The moment didn't last long, though. "I had complete faith in her power, but Soames was resourceful when he needed to be. I was worried that he might find some way of escaping—or worse, of harming her."

"I'll bet the previous owner was completely fooled, wasn't he? Until it was too late."

"Well, no . . . not quite. I knew of the island because I'd been to Lake Languor in my youth. The house was just being built then, and I remember thinking how wonderful it must be to live somewhere like that. The peace, the seclusion, the lack of distractions. To be able to carry out one's work away from the prying eyes of an ignorant, unsympathetic society is a dream. My experiments were increasing in frequency—I admit it's always been an addiction. When the Lady came into my life, I decided it was time to move away from London to a location not only where I could work with complete privacy, but where the Lady could feed without the remains of her meals being discovered.

"I remember the weather was beautiful when I arrived at Tryst that day. I'd visited a few weeks before, to scout out the area and take a look at the island. I doubt Mr. West had noticed me on the occasions I chartered a boat and sailed around the lake taking pictures and watching him when he moved about outside the house. You can build up a pretty good picture of a person's psychological makeup, just by observing them. That day felt right for the business at hand. I made a deal with the harbormaster to keep any other visitors off the water until I'd returned, just to be on the safe side. I had the measure of that man from day one. No morals. His only concern was pleasure. I could tell you things about him you wouldn't believe.

"Anyway, Mr. West was, at the very least, surprised to see me. I think hearing someone at his front door must have been as unsettling as it was unexpected. He appeared after some moments, a look of befuddlement on his old face, and demanded to know what I was doing on his island. I was polite to begin with. I didn't want my business on that day to be unpleasant, and it would have been nice to have moved into the house on a high note. But I had too much trouble getting Mr. West into a position where I could deal with him quickly and painlessly. I told him I had a proposition for him, that I wanted to buy the island for a very high price and would like a tour. The idea was to get him away from the house and take him out quickly. Burying him would have been quite a task, but a small price to pay. Unfortunately, he was most unwelcoming. He kept demanding that I leave the island, trying to shut the door in my face. . . . Eventually I quite lost my temper and pushed the door in, knocking him to the floor of the hall. I—I had the dagger with me. My temper doesn't often get the better of me, you know, but . . . I think Mr. West brought out the worst in me. It was so infuriating that he should make things difficult when they could have been so easy."

Mather looked at his feet, rolling his tongue around his teeth thoughtfully.

"Such is life, I suppose. Once I'd finished with him I dragged his body into the forest and dumped it where it couldn't be found while I returned to London to arrange the move. That's when I found the research center. I pulled his corpse into the building and down into the basement. The pit used to have a ladder that went down to the floor below. At the bottom was a drain that led to the lake, which could be used for disposing of waste. And that's exactly what I did. I pulled the ladder off the wall and pushed his body down there to decompose and fall away into the drain. Perhaps there is still a part of him down there—at the bottom."

"You sick bastard. How could you enjoy killing people like that?" I wanted Mather away from me. He was making my flesh crawl, and I couldn't help wishing I'd made sure that he was dead after pushing him into the pit earlier.

"It occurred to me long ago that what scares us most isn't death, disease or nuclear war. What's most terrifying isn't the world outside, but the world inside." He let this hang in the air awhile. "We are what we see in the mirror. But we are also what we don't see. The organs, the flesh, the . . . gore. But we ignore that because it's horrible. *We* are horrible. You see? Turned inside out we're the most horrific sights imaginable. I've always been fascinated by that. That's why I do it, if you must know. I want to understand why we are so truly abominable once the skin is peeled away."

"You're a lunatic!"

"And you are young, still to understand the complexities of nature."

Mather zipped up his jacket, then walked to the edge of the clearing and into the trees that led down to the beach. I was still baffled. Why did he feel the need to give me all this information? Was he trying to confess? He couldn't possibly be suffering from guilt.

I couldn't hear any noise from the beach. Despite the shadow of doom that lay over my predicament, I still felt detached and slow. Perhaps the blow to the head had deadened my alertness. As I was fighting another wave of nausea, I heard a voice calling me. My eyes closed and I was consumed by a welcoming darkness.

I'm here. It was a female voice again, sweet and beguiling.

"Where?"

Close.

"What do you mean?"

It doesn't matter. Listen to me. You mustn't give in. This will all be over soon.

"I'm not sure I like the sound of that."

You will come to no harm. He will only do what I allow.

"Mather?"

Yes.

"Who are you?"

I am Nhan Diep.

"What? I must be dreaming."

No. You are not even asleep.

To confirm this, I opened my eyes and saw that I was still in the damp clearing. Nothing suggested I was dreaming.

"You can't be the mosquito. That's just not possible."

But it is. I have been in this form for a long time. Thankfully, that will soon end.

"Why?"

Because you are here.

"Me?"

Yes. I've been waiting for you. There was a pause, as though something was holding her back.

He would have killed you in your sleep the first night, if I'd let him. He would end your life right now, but he can't. Though it torments him greatly, he cannot overcome my will.

"But why have you been waiting for me?"

You are very rare, Ashley Reeves.

"Rare?"

I thought I might never find you, but here you are at last. My salvation.

I could hear voices outside my head now, from the direction of the beach. I sensed her presence wane, and before long she was gone.

XII: INCARCERATION

The first voice was undoubtedly Mather's.

"This isn't the time! What the devil's the matter with you?"

"I came to get the boat. He won't be needing it anymore, will he?"

The second voice was familiar, though I couldn't place it to begin with. *Is that Soames?* I thought. Perhaps he'd survived Mather's attack after all. Perhaps Mather had lied to me about killing him. There was a pause, then the same voice, louder.

"This is getting silly, you know. You can't do this forever and expect no one to notice. I'm doing all I can, but I can't keep it up much longer." If it was Soames, he sounded calmer, more self-assured than before.

"The boat was wrecked, so you've had a wasted trip."

Despite the awkwardness and discomfort, I twisted my neck to the left and saw by the light of the moon Mather and the newcomer enter the clearing. They both walked toward the house but stopped halfway there. The second man noticed me. He was surprised, but still managed a weak smile as he turned to Mather. It wasn't Soames after all. It was Derringher, the harbormaster.

"Smashed it up, did he? That'll cost you. What are you going to do with him?"

"What do you think? He's going to help me with my research. Some day soon it'll all pay off. There'll be books written about me, mark my words. You should feel honored to have been given a part in all this. You should be grateful, and it is essential that you continue doing your job, otherwise this will all be for nothing."

At this the other man just shook his head and laughed. It was a hoarse, dirty sound that I didn't like. Mather seemed to feel the same way.

"There'll be books written, all right," the harbormaster said. "You're off your head. And don't think I don't know what you're playing at. You're sick. . . ." His lack of respect for Mather wasn't surprising, yet it caused the other man to round on him.

"Just hold your damned tongue! You've no idea what I've done, what I've discovered. An ignorant fool like you couldn't conceive of the wonders, the miracles the human body has yet to yield. I don't need peasants like you coming here and making a mockery of my life's work. You just do what you're told or you won't get paid."

The other man paused for a while, then turned and grabbed Mather by the collar. "You'd best be the one watching your mouth or I'll be doing some experimenting of my own!" He let the squirming Mather go, pushing him away sharply. "As for getting paid, I want more. A grand for the boat he wrecked, and another two for keeping my trap shut."

"What? A thousand pounds for driftwood? Listen, you! I'm not parting with that kind of money just to fuel your greed."

"Oh, I think you will, my friend."

"Oh, do you?" Mather laughed, something that didn't go down very well with the other man. "You have some sense of humor. Do you think I'm going to just throw money at you every time you ask for it?"

"Yes. I do, as a matter of fact. 'Cos if you don't, I'll have a word with my friend Sergeant Strutt, and I don't think you'd like that."

"You don't intimidate me, you odious man."

"What?"

"Forget it. I'm not explaining everything to you."

"Well then, I might just go and pay our local police station a visit after all. It's not like you've got nothing to hide, is it? They'll have a field day if they come over here." His eyes revealed a gleeful malice. "What do you reckon?"

"Nice try, but I know you only too well. You'll do what I tell you or you won't get another penny."

The electricity in the air was palpable. The two men stood there, staring each other down. Then, unexpectedly, I heard the voice again.

Prepare yourself. This will not be pleasant.

"What?"

If something had triggered the action, I didn't see it. In a flash Mather brandished the wicked dagger and lunged at the harbormaster, stabbing the blade deep into the man's thinly shirted belly. The big fellow just stood

194

there, staring at Mather for a few cold seconds, before looking down at the hand, the knife, and the spreading red stain on his shirt. He began coughing horribly. Mather withdrew the snaking blade as Derringher staggered backward.

I turned to my right and threw up into the grass. Seeing Mather's butchery up close made me realize how near I was to my own demise. I would be next unless I could do something to save myself. *When?* I pleaded. *When will this nightmare end?*

Soon, came the answer. *Very soon.*

I looked back to see Mather rushing toward me. *Oh, my God, she's right, it's going to end now. He's going to kill me.*

But he didn't. He cut through the ropes binding my hands and waist and hauled me to my feet. Pain shot up my legs and for a panicked moment I thought I wouldn't be able to walk. Mather swiftly marched me to the front door, then inside the house. We went past the living room and along the hall to his bedroom. He turned on the light, pushed me down on the floor by the window and tied my hands behind my back again, before turning to leave.

"If you try anything silly, I'll know about it. And I'll make you regret it." He waved the dagger at me, as though I needed convincing.

"Where are you going?"

"I'm going back outside to make Mr. Derringher eat his words—as well as a few other things." A droplet of sweat or rainwater fell from his forehead. "Have you ever wondered, as I have, Mr. Reeves, if a human being is capable of swallowing his own intestines?" With that chilling remark, he left the room, locked the door, then marched back down the corridor to the front of the house. Looking up, I could see that the right-hand panel of the wall had been moved across, revealing the tank. At that moment the insect seemed to be hiding.

I felt ill again, understandably. Mather was indeed a monster, a fiend driven by a perverted sadism. As I pulled at the rope around my wrists I realized how drained I was. Even if it were loose, I doubt I could have done anything about it. Sitting there against the wall, feeling the mud slowly dry on my clothes and body, it was hard not to feel completely hopeless.

I looked up at the tank, and saw that the mosquito had now appeared. My head swam and began to feel very heavy. I thought about the voice I'd heard, the voice claiming to be Nhan Diep. It all seemed so absurd, and I felt foolish for believing it, despite the trauma I'd endured.

"I'm going to pass out," I said to no one in particular. My head fell forward.

Numbness, then an assortment of random images. I could feel her presence again. She was trying to force her way into my head but something was holding her back. I felt as if I were being pushed into a large open space, in absolute darkness. Then she relinquished her hold on me, leaving me confused and cold.

My teeth were chattering now and my neck was aching

because my head had been resting forward on my chest. I looked up and was horrified to see Mather, soaked, standing in the doorway. Then, seeing that he was still holding the dagger in one hand, my breath caught in my throat. It was dripping water and blood onto the floor. I looked him in the eye, trying to gauge his intent. He looked from me to the glass tank, then back again. I had the impression that he was desperate to do something, but wasn't quite ready to take the next step.

"I couldn't help it, could I?" He held up the dagger, wiped the blade with a handkerchief, then laid it on the bed. "It's amazing how quickly lies can become a way of life," he said, staring at the window. I wished he would get on with it instead of toying with me. It was as if something was restraining him, and the fact that he couldn't deal with me was causing him serious stress. He seemed to be breaking down, losing coherent thought and control over the situation.

"I suppose Soames told you everything," Mather said, walking over to the bed and sitting down. "I should never have bullied him so much. It was unfair of me. But the experiments, they—they consumed my mind. It's the excitement, the adventure. After the first time I just couldn't stop."

He was beyond help. I too felt lost; physically and mentally wrecked, and in no condition to fight, or resist. I was at the mercy of the merciless.

"I regret none of it, though," he went on, staring at his feet. "I consider the whole experience a privilege. I've seen things few people could dream of." He then let out the most peculiar and unsettling of laughs and walked over to the tank. "And it's all thanks to her."

"Her?"

"Yes. It was her idea to come here. Here we could continue our work undisturbed by society. I was quite unprepared for the successes that followed. The plan was so simple. We just used her as the bait. We used her to beguile unwitting fools."

"People will miss me. Not just my editor, but my colleagues as well. They'll come for me. I know they will."

"Colleagues are different from friends and relatives. Their concern is generally minimal. They'll have more important things to worry about than you. However, if anyone really did try to track you down, my good friend the harbormaster would be able to—"

"He's dead."

"Oh, yes." Mather had genuinely forgotten. "He is, isn't he? Why did I do that?" He looked at the dagger lying on the bed, then back at the tank. "Why did I do that?" His voice was louder now. The mosquito started making the whining noise again. His eyebrows were raised. "They'll come now. What then? First Soames, now Derringer. Why did you let me do it? Do you want things to fall apart—is that it?" He started walking up and down the room, scratching his head. It was as though, for the first time, he was facing the ramifications of his actions.

"I'm surprised the Lady isn't upset with you for what you've done," I said.

"What?"

I couldn't help but find comedy in Mather's expression. He looked confused and irritated. He also seemed to be developing a nervous twitch.

"Luring all those people to the island and murdering them was a pretty risky business. But now that you've killed Derringher you've really dropped yourself in it. People will notice his disappearance. It's only a matter of time before they come looking for him. And how will she get her blood once you've been locked away? You're her only supplier."

Mather looked at the cage. The Ganges Red was quiet now, but I felt she could hear and understand everything being said.

"She wanted me to do it. I'm sure she did! This doesn't make sense. Why? Why didn't you stop me?" If the mosquito gave him an answer, I didn't hear it. "It won't matter. She'll get her blood. She knows that. I'll solve the Derringher problem. Everything will be as it was."

"No, it won't. People will come here soon. Lots of people. And when they do it'll all be over."

Mather picked up the shining dagger and gazed at the blade. "Not before I've performed one last experiment." He moved his gaze slowly toward me. "Any suggestions, Mr. Reeves?"

I tried to remain calm and assertive, but it was a terrific effort. I must have been shaking all over. "No. None that spring to mind."

"You should hope no one ever finds you, Mr. Reeves—

because I'll kill them if they come. Every last one of them."
He leaped at me, blind insanity in his eyes, a focused expression of the terrible. "I'll kill everyone and everything on this island if I have to, but I won't let them take her!"

I closed my eyes and braced myself for the inevitable.

After some seconds had passed I opened my eyes and looked up to see Mather standing over me, the dagger raised above his head in both hands, wavering. His teeth were gritted; sweat had formed on his brow from the effort he was expending. He was trying very hard to kill me, but once again some force was intervening, thwarting him. He groaned, glared at the insect in her tank, then turned and stormed out. I heard the key in the lock.

My stomach reminded me that I hadn't eaten since breakfast, but asking Mather for food was likely to be a waste of breath. The horror of it all was immense, yet I felt lucky to be alive. I forced myself to stay alert, to listen, to prepare for whatever might transpire. There was little that could be done in my bound state. My legs weren't tied together, but it didn't really matter. I lacked the strength to even stand up. If my wits were all I had, I'd have to keep them sharp.

A few minutes passed, the struggle to stay conscious becoming harder every second, until I heard the sound of running water from the bathroom. Mather was taking a shower. I could hear him muttering to himself. Once or twice he called out some unfamiliar name. He'd murdered Soames and Derringher within an hour of each other, then he'd tried to kill me. He was cracking up. His world was falling apart around him. Something had driven him to despair. Perhaps it had been the dragonfly. He hadn't mentioned the insect since attacking me in the forest, but it had to be on his mind.

My concentration wavered. The mosquito had started flying around the tank, clearly upset by something. Then I heard it: Nhan Diep was invading my thoughts once more. But this time the confidence and serenity were missing from the words.

Why? It sounded almost afraid.

"Why what?"

Why are you thinking about dragonflies?

"None of your business."

Tell me!

"No. You're a figment of my imagination. And I'm tired of having conversations with myself."

See me.

"No!"

See me. Now.

"I don't want to."

Look up.

I looked up.

Now to the left.

My eyes moved once more to the tank, and the Ganges Red. It flicked its wings once, then twice, then: *Now do you see me?*

There was no point in denying it any longer. "OK," I said, almost laughing. "I see you."

Now see me. Truly see me.

I continued to stare at the insect, transfixed now by its appearance. Although it was over in the tank, it seemed to fill my vision. Around it was what looked like television static. Tiny particles of color fizzing around the tank, obscuring anything that might distract my attention.

The Ganges Red, despite my desperate hope that the voice had been imagined, was definitely looking at me. I could feel its gaze. It was unmistakable. And then, as if to remove the doubt in my mind once and for all, the voice came again, this time louder, more insistent, its tone commanding.

I am no figment of your imagination, Ashley Reeves. You know that. I am Nhan Diep!

I could say nothing and could think little more. My body and mind were subdued, controlled somehow. The creature's words were completely implausible, and yet, even in the madness of that moment, I sensed the truth in them.

She continued, *Now, tell me why a dragonfly is on your mind.*

"I don't know," I replied, grinning like a mischievous child. I could feel her attitude change from concern to anger, and in that instant the sound of running water from the bathroom ceased.

XIII: MANIPULATION

Despite the depth of the mess he was in, Mather started whistling. The sound began in the bathroom, then came closer and closer, until I heard the key turn in the lock. The Ganges Red was quiet now and had once more disappeared from view.

The door opened slowly. Mather crept into the room with visible caution. As he closed the door behind him, I noticed that the dagger was now tucked into the belt of his bathrobe. He turned and stood there looking down at me, unsure what to do or say. There was a mixture of emotions in his eyes, which I failed to completely fathom. I could see the fear, however. It was unmistakable. He now viewed me as a threat, an unplanned element of danger. He'd intended to destroy me, and had been denied the kill for reasons he wasn't totally sure of. He still wanted to destroy me—that was obvious—but I think he was afraid of what would happen if he tried again. He was stuck with me now. And he had no idea of how to proceed.

"You really want me dead, don't you?" The words sprang from my mouth almost of their own accord. I'd only meant to think them.

Mather didn't answer; instead, he walked over to the recess and drew the panel across. He did it slowly, never once taking his eyes off me, worried, as unlikely as it was, that I would somehow be able to attack him.

"You'd prefer it if I just died right now and made things easier for you. I tell you what," I said, feeling for perhaps the first time that I had some control. "Why don't you untie me, give me the dagger, and I'll do the job myself."

His expression remained unchanged. I started laughing softly. Mather was unimpressed. His hand wavered over the hilt of the dagger.

"You would do well to watch yourself right now, my friend." He began moving away from the panel. "I shall be back presently." He left, returning a few minutes later dressed in clean clothes. The dagger was now hidden somewhere, no doubt still within reach.

"Up," he said. I was unsure I'd heard correctly, as I hadn't seen his lips move. Then, unmistakably this time: "Up! On your feet!" He moved a couple of steps toward me.

"I can't." This was true. My body was nothing but an unresponsive sack of flesh and bone. My energy was spent. "I can hardly talk, let alone move."

Once again the dagger was produced and pointed at me. "No time for games."

"No time for games? There was plenty of time before! Isn't that what you like to do? Play games with people?"

Mather walked forward another step. "Get up now!"

"You'll have to help me." I watched him fidget nervously,

204

still uncomfortable with the situation. He didn't want to help me up. I don't think he even wanted to touch me. "Believe me, I don't have the strength to put up a fight."

"Yes, well, you'll forgive me if I don't give you the benefit of the doubt."

"I'll just have to stay here, then, won't I?"

"You will go to the spare room! I need to be alone to decide what to do."

I thought about it and realized I'd probably be better off in the other room. I'd be away from him, away from that creature, and I'd be somewhere I could get my head clear. With some effort, using the wall and window ledge behind me for support, I was able to struggle to my feet.

I leaned against the window for some time, summoning the strength to move. Mather continued to point the knife at me, keeping me at bay. My head began throbbing again, bringing tears to my eyes. I still had no idea of the damage Mather had done to my skull. For all I knew the wound could prove to be fatal. Mather sneered, as though I were putting on some pathetic act for him. This made me shake my head.

"You only had to hit me a little harder, and you could have finished me there in the forest."

"I didn't hit you that hard. It's nothing."

"Oh, it's more than nothing," I spat, "believe me."

"Just move, will you?"

"I'm moving." I pushed myself away from the window and staggered across to the door. Mather kept his distance, but stayed alert in case I made a foolhardy dash for freedom. I assumed Derringher had come to the island by boat, but I didn't have time to waste looking for where he'd moored it. If I had the chance I had to go for the tunnel in the forest. But I couldn't get there without incapacitating Mather first, which would prove extremely difficult with my hands tied.

I nudged the door open with my right shoulder and was about to enter the corridor when Mather grabbed my arm, halting me.

"Wait."

"What is it?"

"Shh!" He was still looking at me, but his attention was diverted. He seemed to be listening. After a few seconds I could hear something above the endless pounding in my head. It was the sound of a motor. And it was getting louder.

Mather pulled me back into the room and pushed me against the window. I caught sight of my reflection. It was shocking: the face staring back at me was almost unrecognizable. The hair was wild and matted. It stuck to my forehead in clumps, glued there with drying mud. Dirt, leaves and other forest debris covered my clothes. He must have dragged rather than carried me to the clearing. I looked terrible. Mather walked over to the panel, pulled it back across and stood in front of the glass tank, muttering some words I was unable to catch. He then did something completely unthinkable. He lifted the lid.

Placing the heavy brass panel on the floor, he turned to me and smiled at the look of sheer horror on my face.

"I shall be leaving you in the Lady's care while I go and see to our unexpected guest. Naturally, if you try to scream or do anything similarly foolish, she will have to take action."

"You can't leave me alone with her!" Panic once more consumed me.

"I'm afraid I have to. Now, if you'll excuse me." Mather turned and left; he pulled the door behind him but it failed to close properly. I was unable to take my eyes from the tank, and, as I watched, the insect rose slowly from the confines of the glass box and hovered toward me.

Please . . . sit.

I sat on the edge of the bed as instructed. The mosquito floated over to the desk and landed. Her wings rose and fell hypnotically, as I'd seen them do before. The rest of her body was still, and appeared almost brown now.

Do you remember what we spoke of earlier?

"Something about the end coming. About you not letting him harm me."

That's right. I will protect you.

"He tried to kill me earlier."

Yes, and I told you—he tried while you were asleep last night, and after he had attacked you in the forest. I could have stopped him from hurting you at all, but I couldn't allow you to get away.

It was deeply sobering to think that I could so easily have been dead already; that Mather would have slaughtered me quite happily without the mosquito to stop him.

"So why didn't you let him kill me?"

You are important to me. You have something I've been looking for.

"I'm more important to you than Mather?"

Mather only lives because he has been useful.

"How was he useful?"

Blood.

"But why do you need it? You can't reproduce, can you?"

No . . .

I could detect no element of sadness in her voice. It seemed that reproduction was no concern of hers.

"So why do you need it?"

There was a slight pause, then: *I have an unquenchable thirst for it.*

"And Mather has been able to provide you with enough?"

He has provided me with plenty. When I found him, I knew immediately that he would be a willing servant. That night in London I was searching, as I had for so many nights before, for new blood. In the city I couldn't do the killing myself, as I could sometimes leave a mess. It was hard to control my thirst, and I didn't want to risk leaving a trail that might lead to my capture. The thought of incarceration is intolerable. I have to be free, or with a companion who knows my requirements and is willing to help me. Mather proved to be such an accomplice. I could smell the many-layered blood of his experiments from far off. When I entered the house, the scent was maddening. I threw myself against the door of the chamber until they let me in.

Once inside the room I knew I had found someone I could use. It didn't take long to gain control of Mather's mind. He was an easy puppet. I convinced him, with little effort, to increase the frequency of his experiments, to keep the blood supply at a satisfactory level. As each experiment passed, his fascination for the macabre grew. The darkness inside him was eating away at his soul, destroying his sense of right and wrong. Soon he was experimenting every night—not just to please me, but to satisfy his own lust for mutilation.

"What about Soames? Did he ever try to stop you?"

I quickly asserted my influence over him, but with intimidation rather than control. I gave him plenty of examples of what would happen if he were ever to cross me, or interfere with Mather's work. When we finally moved here, I thought things would be perfect. Mather's enthusiasm for the experiments increased, and the blood flowed in abundance.

"It's all about to end, though."

Yes. Nothing can stop it now. And it's all because of you.

"Me?"

Your coming here was the beginning of the end.

"For everyone?"

No. Not everyone.

She sounded surprised, as if I'd said something ridiculous. I remembered what she'd said before about not letting Mather harm me. I couldn't think why she was so determined to keep me alive. I assumed I'd be no more than food to her.

"Why are you so concerned about my well-being?"

I was human once, and I betrayed the one I loved. Because of that betrayal I was cursed.

"Ngoc Tam."

Yes. He was my husband. He—he couldn't bear to live without me. His blood brought me back from the grave, and in return I deserted him for a richer man and a life of luxury. For so long now I have traveled the world, searching for his blood, so that I might be human once more.

I could guess what was coming, as implausible as it was.

"But surely your husband's blood was unique. Surely no blood but his could restore you."

His family were travelers. They must have spread all over the world. His descendants are likely to exist in vast numbers today. I knew I would come across one of them eventually. And now I have. When I first smelled your blood, I knew it was his. So unique and potent. I was excited beyond measure. My prayers have finally been answered. When the time is right, when we are completely alone, I shall drink . . . and I shall be yours.

I started shivering, and not because it was cold in the room.

When I had all but relinquished hope, I found what my heart craved. In your veins flows the blood of my old love, Ngoc Tam.

"No, that's not—"

Your bloodline goes back—

"But—"

Generations apart, but still strong. With Tam's blood the curse will be lifted, and I will no longer be contained in this loathsome form, a slave to the bloodlust. Please believe that I have no desire to harm you. All I need is a few drops of blood.

"So the legend is true. No wonder you were worried about the dragonfly."

The dragonfly? You were thinking about it because you have read one of Mather's books. Ha! I was worried for nothing.

"No." I smiled. "I was thinking about it because it's here on the island. The genie is here. He's come for you."

Shh . . . Don't lie—it is pointless.

"It's true! Mather knows as well. The genie has found you and I think he intends to stop you becoming a woman again."

Even if he really is here, he won't stop me. Nothing can stop me now. I won't allow it!

Just then I heard voices. With a great effort I managed to get back on my feet. Looking through the window, in the moonlight I saw them walking to the right of the house, heading for the path that led into the woods. I couldn't quite see who Mather was with at first, but he seemed to be leading someone toward the research center. I could just make out what he was saying:

". . . hard at work taking pictures. I know it's late but he wanted to get as many as he could before he left tomorrow."

Then I heard her voice. Beautiful, yet so terrifying

because it was so out of place here in this dark theater of horror.

"Oh, right . . . I had to just take a boat from the harbor back at the town. I hope it's OK, I couldn't find anyone—"

"Not to worry. I know the harbormaster well. I'm sure he won't mind."

"Ash called me earlier and we got cut off. It sounded like he was having trouble . . ." And then her voice faded away.

"Gina! Oh, God, no! Please," I implored. "You have to stop him. You have to—"

It's pointless.

"No!" I struggled with the rope binding my wrists, but the effort was futile. Mather had done too good a job. "I've got to . . . He'll kill her."

It was the most distressing agony. I had to get out of that room and protect her. The thought of her alone with him was more than I could bear.

"I have to stop him."

Shh, my love. In a while she will be gone. Then there will be nothing to cause you pain. Your suffering can only exist while she is alive.

"You could do something. You have control over him."

Yes, I do.

"Then use it!"

No. Her life is of no interest to me. She merely provides a necessary distraction.

"What?"

While he is preoccupied with her, I will take what I need from you. I think Mather has grown too accustomed to me, but now is the time for me to leave. It is better for him to be elsewhere when I transform. I don't want him trying to interfere.

"No. Don't do this, please."

I understand that you are scared. But it will not hurt.

"Please!"

You are weak. You should rest now.

"So you can drink me dry? I don't think so."

I have no wish to be so cruel.

"All right—look, you can have my blood, but please save Gina first. She doesn't deserve this, she doesn't deserve to be anywhere near him. Promise me . . . promise me you'll—"

I don't want all your blood, just a drop or two.

"If you become a woman again, you'll still need protection against the genie. If you help Gina, I promise to take care of you."

I could sense her thinking the matter over. She was unsure, nervous. I think she believed I was serious about the presence of the genie, but I didn't know if she accepted that he was capable of stopping her from taking what she wanted.

I must have your blood. I have waited for too long to be denied it now. Both the girl and the genie are irrelevant!

The mosquito hovered in the air almost silently, then settled back on the desk. I really had no idea what she might do. Just as I thought the tension was about to break,

I heard the sound of something moving outside. The Ganges Red turned toward the window and tensed herself. I sensed for the first time a great fear within her. At that moment she was no longer a monster, but a frail creature facing the very real prospect of her own demise.

XIV: SALVATION

If something had been outside, it failed to show itself. After a couple of minutes of muted apprehension we were able to turn and face each other once more. Nhan Diep said nothing to begin with. She may have been mulling things over, but I had the distinct feeling there was something else. Her wings began moving faster; then before I knew it they were vibrating and lifting her into the air once more. She moved across the room to the window and hovered just underneath the sash, looking out into the night. She was no longer broadcasting her thoughts, unwilling, it seemed, to let me hear what she was thinking. She turned slightly, then—before I could react—flew straight at my exposed neck.

I couldn't move. Whether it was the fear or the powerful influence she exerted over my body, I don't know. Either way, she had me at her mercy. Her feeding tube, long, glistening and sharp, could be beneath my skin in less than a second. I couldn't actually see her at this point, as she was under my chin, but I could feel her. A harsh humming came from her legs, and I felt the odd brush of air whenever her wings flapped. I was thankful when at last she broke the silence between us.

I understand how you feel. You long for this woman because you believe she will complete you. The only way of easing the pain in your soul, of filling the emptiness in your heart, is to know that the love you feel for her is returned. That is the truth, is it not?

I couldn't move my lips to speak. Maybe it was because I was still paralyzed by the shock of the mosquito's proximity; maybe because of the way she had summed up my feelings in a few simple sentences. Whichever, I had never felt so vulnerable in my life.

I can offer you an alternative, however. Once she has gone, I can take her place. Your blood is that of my husband's. You would be an ideal mate. If you give up your blood freely, I will give myself to you.

"I'm not giving up on her. There must still be a way—"

Mather will kill her. You must know that.

I think I did know it deep down, and had been trying very hard to ignore it. There was little or nothing I could do to help her. On the other hand, I knew there was a chance that everything Mather had told me about the mosquito's ability to kill could be wrong. She could be harmless, but then again how could something so oversized and colorful be anything but deadly? I couldn't stand the thought of Mather touching Gina, and I couldn't help her if I was drained of blood, my flesh dissolving into liquid. My only hope lay in putting the mosquito out of action long enough to free myself and get away. And I would have to act soon. The look I'd seen on Mather's face before he and Gina had slipped out of sight was one of eagerness, impatience.

It will be so much better if you stop fighting me. Be still, let me in. You've no reason to be afraid anymore. I shall not harm you. . . .

Her voice was utterly bewitching. For a brief moment I was convinced that the best thing I could do was to just forget my troubles and submit to her seduction. It would be so easy, so effortless. In a terrible way I actually began to find her presence comforting. My head no longer ached, the panic had left me, to be replaced by a growing calm. It didn't occur to me that she was manipulating my mind, but if it had I might not have cared. I was feeling better and better by the second. What finally wrenched me from the deepening stupor was the thought of Gina, which washed away the insect's influence in one mighty stroke. At once the pain and the torment returned, and the mosquito's hold was broken.

"Please, just get her off this island alive. After that you can do what you want with me."

She started laughing then, a sound I really didn't like. It sounded dry and old, and seemed to hint at the centuries she'd spent roaming the earth.

You must stop this foolishness or I may be forced to kill you, and I don't want to do that.

Her voice resounded in my head, holding me, fixing my thoughts. The pain began to subside once more. But this time, when I tried to think of Gina, I couldn't quite picture her face. It was as though the mosquito were blocking my efforts, distorting my memories. I started panicking, concentrating hard on bringing her to mind, but my energy was rapidly dwindling. The insect wasn't just numbing the pain and frustration, she was also sapping my strength, my will. I was being reduced to a vegetable, a subdued prisoner in my own body. I was aware that I had started moaning, though it sounded as if it were coming from someone else. She was saying something to me. She may have been singing—it was hard to tell—but it was so soothing, so placating that I didn't want her to stop . . . ever.

And just when I thought I'd never have to worry about anything ever again, I heard something trying to push its way through the narrow space between the door and the frame. I opened my heavy eyelids to see the gap widening and a small shape emerging into the room. It padded across the floor to the bottom of the bed near my feet. I carefully moved my gaze down and saw the cat looking from me to the mosquito on my neck. I was surprised to hear the insect continuing its melodic chant. It couldn't have heard Mr. Hopkins's entrance.

Even though I had seen it, what happened next came as a complete shock. The cat sprang into the air, straight for me, its right forepaw catching the mosquito and hooking it by one of its wings. The two of them went flying off my chest and onto the floor. The spell broke instantly. With an effort I hauled myself to my feet and went straight to the open door, nudging my way round it as fast as I could. I found the front door closed but not locked. Gripping the catch with my teeth, I managed to get it open, terrified all the while that I'd hear the frantic whine of the mosquito behind me. In a second I was out in the cold night, and with renewed energy I tore across the clearing to the path, not daring to look behind. And as if fate hadn't dealt me enough blows already, my foot thumped into a rock, my ankle twisted and I went flying forward onto my face.

My cheeks were hot and stinging, but thankfully my nose wasn't broken. Bits of dirt and grit had embedded themselves in my forehead, but I was otherwise unhurt. Turning over, I managed to get myself into a sitting position. I searched for the rock in the moonlight, and managed to locate it about a meter behind me. One side of it looked particularly sharp, so I turned my back to it and used it to saw at the rope binding my hands. It took a good few minutes to do the job, but I knew I'd be little help to Gina unless my hands were free. I gasped in relief when the rope was finally shredded, and threw the bonds away before getting to my feet. My arms ached badly, and as I stood a pain shot up my right leg. The ankle had been twisted, and I had a horrible feeling that it was no simple injury. I managed to walk, and after a few seconds was able to jog, albeit awkwardly. The pain was awful, but there was no time to take it easy. Gina's life hung in the balance.

I made it to the gate faster than I'd expected. I reached into the foliage on one side and located the spring-loaded bolt, drawing it back and swinging the gate wide open. There was no need to close it—I needed to keep the escape route clear for later.

The darkened research center was a ghost in the nighttime. If it had looked this bad the first time I'd found it, I would never have gone in. It seemed warped by a foul, infernal sickness. Knowing what awaited me inside, entering was a horrifying prospect. But the thought of leaving Gina with Mather a second longer was far worse. I moved forward, swearing as the pain in my foot reasserted itself. I took one final breath of fresh air, then hobbled into the building, allowing its nightmare darkness to swallow me whole.

The hall was nothing but gray and black shapes. Mather could have been hiding anywhere. The only sound was the crunch of glass under my feet as I hobbled toward the other end. I thought I could see a faint light around the basement door, but it was hard to be certain. I made my uncomfortable way over to it, listening carefully for any sounds.

He had tried to close the door, but being so stiff it had only jammed against the frame. With some effort, trying all the while not to make any noise, I pushed the door inward. Looking down the stairwell, I could now see a flickering light at the bottom. They were down there. Grabbing the handrail to support some of my weight, I took the stairs carefully.

When I reached the bottom I heard Gina cry out. She sounded shocked, scared, and angry, but at least she was alive. My head seemed to clear a little. I crept to the doorway of the theater and slowly peered round.

I could only see Mather. He had his back to me, and was standing by the lip of the pit, one hand holding the dagger, the other by his side. A lamp was placed by his right foot, spilling light into the opening. He must have been watching Gina, though what she was doing in the pit I couldn't tell. Then there was a bright flash, and it became clear that she was taking photographs for him. He didn't intend to let us leave the island, so why have pictures taken when he could come to the pit whenever he liked? Maybe he wanted a record of his work to survive, long after the bodies had decomposed. But as the mosquito had pointed out, Mather's time would soon be up. Gina and I wouldn't go unmissed. Eventually the authorities would come to the island. It was possible that Mather wanted to be remembered. The photographs might represent peace of mind for him, a way of assuring him that the world would see what he had done, that he would not be forgotten. It could have been as simple, as vain and as crazy as that. I could hear what sounded like sobbing. I knew what Gina could see and smell down there. I had to get her out.

Time was a factor. I didn't know how long Mather's patience would last, but I knew it would run out eventually, possibly quite soon. Another flash went off, causing Mather to flinch and rub his eyes for a second or two afterward. This was something I could use to my advantage. Shaking with nerves, I waited for the next flash. It was impossible to warn Gina, or move farther into the room in case I made a sound and gave myself away. The light bloomed, and as Mather lifted his hand to rub his eyes, I ran straight at him.

The pain was as surprising as it was terrible. I was moving fast, and the impact jarred and moved my ankle about, possibly causing further damage. Nevertheless, I banged Mather hard with my shoulder, throwing him forward into the pit. He hit the wall opposite with his head before crashing onto the pile of bodies below. It was the second time I had sent him down there and, I prayed, the last. I was greatly relieved to see that he hadn't landed on Gina. It had been a risk I'd had to take. He was lying on his side atop the bodies, moaning. The dagger was nowhere to be seen. I looked down at Gina, her features thrown into sharp relief by the light from the lamp, which had remained in place by the doorway. She looked at me, then at the crumpled body of Mather, then climbed over two or three corpses until she was standing below the doorway. I dropped to the floor, trying not to put any weight on my ankle, and reached down for her hands. I hoisted her up and into the room.

"Are you OK?"

"Oh, God. Oh, my God!" She was shaking as she reached out and hugged me. "What the hell's going on?"

"Come on, let's get out of here." I turned to leave, but Gina stopped to look back down into the pit at Mather's tangled form.

"Shouldn't we . . . do something about him?" She swung the camera around her neck.

"What do you mean?"

"Well, do you think he's dead?"

"I don't know, we haven't got time—"

"We can't just leave him. He'll come after us."

"I'm not killing anyone . . . and neither are you."

"That pit . . ." I could see the tears in her eyes. "Do you know what's down there?"

"Yes, I do . . . All right look, give me a hand with this," I said, rushing around the side of the operating table and taking a firm grip. Thankfully, with some effort I could feel it budge. Gina took the other side and we turned the table so that the narrow end was facing the doorway.

"On top of him?" Gina asked, her eyes bright white circles in the gloom.

"Yeah." We both pushed hard, noticing the dried blood peeling off the floor in sheets as we moved. The table teetered on the threshold, then with one final shove, it slid forward and down onto the bodies below. There was a loud thud and Mather screamed. Without further hesitation, we turned and fled.

I led the way up the steps as fast as my ankle would allow. Gina insisted on supporting me, pointing out that a fall back down to the basement wouldn't improve our situation. I had to agree, but I couldn't help feeling that I was hindering what could be our only chance of escape.

Thankfully, we were fast and were across the main hall in no time. We reached the porch and froze. From behind and below us came another hideous, inhuman scream. An angry, cheated bellowing, so loud it seemed unreal. Mather was furious. Judging by that awful primal roar, I imagined he would gladly tear the limbs from our bodies, given the opportunity.

We turned and ran out of the porch and onto the forest path. I insisted I could move unaided, and despite the pain I managed to keep up a good pace.

"So, what did he do to you?" Gina asked as we tore along.

"He hit me with a shovel."

"Oh."

When we arrived back at the house, it was disturbingly quiet. I could see no sign of the mosquito or the cat. Gina pulled my arm and I followed her in the direction of the beach, and her boat. If we were lucky, we might just make it.

As we came to the start of the path that led through the trees to the beach, I heard a voice in my head. I stopped and grabbed Gina's jacket, halting her progress. We both looked back toward the house and saw the small humming demon approach.

Take one more step, and I'll kill her!

XV: DISASSOCIATION

There was nothing I could do. We both stood rooted to the spot as the insect approached. Running would have been pointless. There was nowhere it couldn't follow. The monster stopped in front of us and hovered in the air, twitching its head from side to side. It didn't seem to have been harmed by Mr. Hopkins's attack.

"What . . . is that?"

"It's a very . . . dangerous . . . insect."

What do you think you're doing with her? She should be dead!

"I had to save her. You must understand—"

I do not understand! It makes no sense! I should kill her right here and now. Perhaps when you see her lifeless body dissolving away into the earth, you will see how utterly meaningless she is.

"Just let us go. Please." I was still fighting the fatigue that plagued my body. My energy was again ebbing fast, along with my resistance to the mosquito's persuasion.

"What are you doing?" Gina had spoken to me, though her eyes were still fixed on the Ganges Red.

"I . . . I'm talking to it."

"What? But it's—"

"Yes, it's hard to explain, but it can communicate with me."

"How?"

"I don't know—it just can."

"You're imagining things," she said.

Oh, don't you start, I thought. "Please, just believe me. It's not like other insects."

"I can see that. But I don't think—"

"Please. Humor me." I looked into her eyes. "Our lives depend on it."

"Don't forget that creep in the pit. He could be on his way here right now."

"Him we can deal with. This one could be a little trickier."

So Mather is alive?

"Just about," I said.

Gina turned to me, shaking her head. She must have thought I was delirious. "Look, we really need to get going," she said. "Regardless of how dangerous that thing is."

You are not leaving! If you value the life of this woman, you will remain on the island.

I looked at Gina, who returned my gaze, as if trying to read my thoughts.

"If we stay, what'll happen to her?"

The insect was silent for a while, thinking of a response.

Gina whispered to me, "What are you doing?"

"We're trying to come to some sort of arrangement."

"Look, I don't understand what's going on, but right

now I don't care. Ash, we *have* to get off this island. That maniac could come back any second and kill us!"

"Look, trust me. This is something beyond our understanding. We have to be very careful."

"How dangerous is it?"

"If she gets her feeding tube into you, she can inject a toxic saliva that'll dissolve the flesh around the wound."

Gina said nothing, but merely stared openmouthed at the mosquito.

That's good. Make her fear me.

"So," I began, facing the Ganges Red. "What will happen to her?"

I am considering it.

I thought of lunging for the creature. Maybe there was I chance I could crush her in my hands before she could retaliate. I didn't like the idea of getting her saliva all over me, but it might be the only way to stop her from attacking Gina. She wouldn't be expecting me to take such drastic action. But then, as if to remind me that she could read my thoughts, she flew up into the air and over our heads, stopping behind us.

Into the house! Now!

It was clear to me then that any attempt to surprise her would be fruitless. She would be aware of my plans almost as soon as I was. There was no other option. I had to do as she said.

"Come on," I said to Gina, the desperation no doubt evident in my voice. "We're going inside."

"What? This is ridiculous!"

"Please, just trust me. There's no choice."

"Ash, for God's sake, come on," she said, turning back toward the beach. "We're going now, even if I have to bloody drag you!"

The mosquito darted at Gina's face, just missing her with its feeding tube. Gina screamed and ran into my arms.

Watch her—or next time I'll give her more than just a warning.

"All right, all right," I said, holding a hand out at the mosquito. "Gina, please, just trust me. I won't let her harm you." We returned to the house in silence, the Ganges Red following close behind.

I had hoped never to see the interior of that building again. It seemed strangely different when we walked inside. The shadows appeared denser, more secretive, the light less substantial. From the look on Gina's face, it was clear that she shared my discomfort.

The mosquito instructed me to lead Gina into Mather's bedroom, perhaps because she herself felt more comfortable there. This was, after all, her home, her sanctuary. I sat on the bed next to Gina, while the Ganges Red hovered in the air before us. I could see no sign of Mr. Hopkins. The struggle must have ended elsewhere in the house.

I watched the mosquito for a short while, trying to gauge her intent, then asked, "What now?" Gina looked across at me, even though she knew I was addressing the insect.

I'm sorry. But this has to be done.

"No!" I had to be mindful of what I was saying. Gina was unsettled enough; it would be so easy to make things worse.

It is the only way.

"Please. Whatever you think might happen between us—it'll never work."

At this, the insect laughed, then hovered closer to me. Gina's face contorted into an expression of complete incredulity. I could only guess at the thoughts that were going through her mind.

Perhaps, but I have the gift of persuasion. In time you will see things my way, and you will love me.

"You're wrong. You can't force someone to love you."

You underestimate me. Everything Mather has done since I found him has been by my direction. You are both strong-minded men, but as his mind bent to my will, so will yours. If I want you to love me—then you shall!

"Not while I draw breath, I won't."

At this she just laughed again.

"What's going on?" Gina had been straining to hear something. Perhaps she thought I was sane after all.

"A disagreement."

"What?"

"Oh, nothing."

"Nothing, my arse! Why are you talking to it?"

"It wants me."

"What?"

"It's hard to explain."

"Is this thing going to hurt us or not?"

"Not if I can help it."

You cannot save her. You may as well tell her the truth. She will be dead soon.

"You won't touch her!" I blurted it out, and straight-away cursed my stupidity.

"Ash," Gina said. "Look, I think that blow to the head has confused you. You're not thinking straight—and I'm not surprised—but—"

"It's all right. Just leave it to me." I tried to think of a way out of the situation. The Ganges Red was silent. I didn't want to tell Gina the truth, but I lacked the energy to lie to her. Given the surreal nature of our predicament, though, it was unlikely that she would believe me anyway. But I had to say something.

"Well." I breathed deeply.

"Hey," she said, taking my right hand in hers. "It's OK. I know you've been through a lot."

I stared her straight in the eyes. "Yes." I smiled. "But you're still not going to like it." Something landed softly on one of the windowpanes. I didn't take any notice to begin with; neither did Gina or the mosquito. I supposed it must have been a leaf or something. "Look, I know how crazy this sounds, but you're just going to have to humor me. You see, that thing wants to kill you because she thinks she's destined to be with me."

Gina's eyes widened even more. "Oh."

"I know, it's ridiculous."

"Well . . . it's going to take some beating, that's for sure."

"There's a possibility that once she drinks my blood she'll become a woman again."

"A woman! My God! Can you hear yourself? Wake up! We really have to get out of here, Ash. We haven't got time for this." She made to stand up, but I grabbed her arm firmly, pulling her back down onto the bed. The mosquito buzzed angrily at her.

"Look," I told her. "I believe it. Well, bits of it . . . I think."

"OK," she said, clearly not believing any of it. "So why does it need your blood?"

"She says I'm a descendant of her late husband. I carry his blood, and she needs his blood to lift the curse."

"I see. . . ."

"She thinks that once she's human again, we can be together . . . as a couple." I didn't have to look at Gina to know what expression she was wearing.

"And it wants to kill me because it thinks I'm the competition?"

"Yes."

"Well, I'm glad that's cleared up. The first thing we need to do when we get back home is take you to a doctor." She looked toward the window. "Is that thing a friend of the mosquito's?"

"What?" I followed her gaze to the window and saw it for the first time. Attached to the glass, looking straight into the room at the three of us, was a huge dragonfly. It was slightly smaller than the Ganges Red, but no less striking.

Only then, when she realized she had lost our attention, did the mosquito turn to face the window. Almost instantly there was a reaction. She darted backward like a bullet and hit the wall by the door, then dropped to the carpet, thrashing about for a second or two, as though trying to regain her senses. She then rose into the air and faced the window again, this time positioning herself farther from the glass.

No . . . not now!

She continued to scream, but this time in a language that made no sense to me. She zipped about the room, unable to keep herself steady. The dragonfly remained motionless. It could have been an ornament for all the life it displayed. Then, as if hearing my thoughts, it detached itself from the glass, its wings humming into life, and moved away from the house, to hover some meters away. The mosquito's scream grew louder and louder until it became a high-pitched whistle. I looked at Gina, who was rubbing her ears. Then suddenly the window shattered, spraying the two of us with thousands of tiny shards. Instinctively we turned away, worried that the glass would shred our faces, but thankfully, we were unharmed. We stood, while the Ganges Red continued screaming her distress. She had been caught in the blast of the glass shower. A red liquid was now oozing from one side of her abdomen. I looked through the hole in the window at the dragonfly outside, convinced that it was watching me. Then I heard a voice, a voice more commanding, more insistent than the mosquito's. It spoke only one word, but it was enough to spur me into action.

Go.

I grabbed Gina's coat sleeve and hauled her with me as I made for the door. We had almost made it to the threshold when the Ganges Red flew across to hover before us, still dripping blood onto the carpet. She held her position with what seemed to be a great effort, proving how desperate she was to keep us under her control.

Get back! Away from the door!

"No. It's over. We're going."

You're going nowhere. I haven't waited this long to be cheated!

"He won't let you get what you want. He's been on this island watching you for some time now. If he wants to put an end to this tonight, he will."

I won't let him! I—

Looking over my shoulder, I saw that the dragonfly had now entered the room. It remained close to the window, moving up and down slightly, its attention concentrated on us. Suddenly the Ganges Red started shrieking again, and fell to the carpet, twisting this way and that.

Go!

I looked down at the Ganges Red as I moved to the door. Gina lifted her foot up as it moved in front of her, and gritted her teeth.

"No! Don't do it!"

"Why not? I can kill it right now!"

"No. It's not up to us. That dragonfly has come for her—let him do it." I pulled on her arm to get her moving, and she followed me out of the room.

Instants later we were heading down the hall. Behind us I could hear the mosquito squealing from the pain of its injuries and the torture the dragonfly was inflicting. It could only be a matter of time before the killing blow was delivered. I followed Gina out into the night, heading straight across the clearing in the direction of the beach and her boat.

Looking up, I could see that the sky was clear. I hoped there would be no more rain, no more rough weather, so that we could get across the lake unimpeded. The nightmare had to end soon. The island's horrors had already taken their toll on me, and I was worried that my mental health was in jeopardy.

We attacked the trees in our fury to get through, not even bothering to stick to the rough trail. I heard the fire before I saw it: it made loud cracking sounds as the wood buckled and snapped. Then, once we were through the trees and on the slope leading down to the beach, we could see the wild conflagration.

"*Nooo!*" Gina screamed, filling the night with her chilling indignation. The two boats, Gina's and the harbormaster's, were now some fifty meters from shore, both aflame. They seemed to be drawn toward each other, as if feeding some joint fury. Even if we could have reached

234

them, it would have been useless by now. My heart sank even further.

"There's another boat on the island," I said, trying not to sound too defeated. "It's Mather's. I don't know where it is, but I'm sure we can find it." I was panicking. I knew the tunnel might have been a better option, but if Mather was after us, he'd be coming from the direction of the forest.

"This can't be happening! I knew we should have come straight here. Look where your whole Dr. Dolittle talking-to-the-bloody-animals routine has got us!"

I had a horrible feeling that at any moment the terror, as though a monster itself, would consume us both.

"All right, I'm sorry, let's just try and make our way round the outside of the island. We'll have to be careful—but I can't think of any other way—"

Suddenly my words were cut off by the sound of laughter.

"Oh dear, oh dear," Mather said, emerging from the cover of the tree line behind us, where he'd been hiding. "What the devil are you to do now, Mr. Reeves? You seem to be finding yourself in predicament . . . after predicament." He just stood grinning at us, his face and clothes filthy from the grime and gore he'd no doubt disturbed during his fall into the pit. The look of glee and childish mischief on his face made me furious.

I walked toward him, feeling the frustration within me turning to anger. In that instant I no longer cared about any knife he might be carrying. I meant to hurt him, and there was nothing he could do about it.

"I've had enough! You hear me? Enough!" I curled my hands into fists, ready to strike.

But as always, Mather's confidence was justified. I don't know where he'd been hiding it, but just then he raised a large shotgun and leveled it at me.

"Please. Calm yourself. And I'd prefer you both to keep your distance, if you don't mind."

Gina and I exchanged glances. There seemed to be no way out of this living hell.

Mather marched us back through the trees to the clearing, then ordered us to stop. From where we stood we could see the left side of the house. Glass was twinkling on the ground in the light from Mather's bedroom.

"What happened to the window?" He moved round to our left.

I smiled. "While the lovely Scarlet Lady was entertaining us, we had an unexpected visitor."

Mather's face twisted into a look of disgust. He grunted in disappointment. "Moth-eaten ratbag! I'll throttle that mangy thing's neck!"

"If you're referring to Mr. Hopkins, he wasn't the one who broke the window."

Mather looked across at me. "Then who did?"

"Who's Mr. Hopkins?" Gina looked from me to Mather.

"He's a cat."

"Oh."

"Well? Who was it?" Mather was getting angry now.

"The dragonfly. He—"

"Dragonfly? Pah! You're lying."

"No, I'm not. Go and see for yourself. Before we left, your precious Lady was fighting for her life."

"No!"

"Yes," Gina replied.

Just then something flew out the front door. It was smaller than before, and looked drained, deflated even. It flew straight at Mather, emitting an ear-piercing shriek.

Mather was stunned. His beautiful specimen had been badly, possibly fatally, wounded. He kept the shotgun pointed squarely at Gina and me, but his eyes were on the approaching insect.

"Oh, my Lady," he said. "Whatever has happened?"

The genie! Tien Thai! He has come for me.

"No."

Yes! It's your fault for opening the tank. He wouldn't have been able to get to me otherwise. Now you're going to help me defeat him.

The red monster hovered before Mather, studying his face, perhaps seeking answers.

"But I don't know if I can kill it. I—"

Your blood. I must have it now. It is the only way.

I wondered then why she didn't just take *my* blood. But if she thought she'd become a woman again by drinking my blood, perhaps this would make her vulnerable to the dragonfly.

"No!" Mather stepped back, visibly shaken, and aimed the shotgun at the insect.

What do you think you're doing? Point that away from me, fool!

Somewhat reluctantly, Mather did as he was told.

I won't hurt you. I'll just take what I need to recover my strength.

"I don't . . . I don't want to."

Don't want to what?

"I don't want to give you my blood."

What are you talking about? I told you, it won't hurt. Now tie these two up while we deal with the dragonfly.

"Why can't I kill them? It's pointless to—"

You will not kill them!

"What about the girl? Surely you don't need her alive! Take *her* blood."

I need him to be compliant. She needs to be unharmed— at least for now. . . .

This last remark stung, but it was hardly unexpected. I knew the Ganges Red would try to remove Gina at some point. I just hoped I'd be ready at the critical moment.

"What's going on?"

I had forgotten that Gina couldn't hear the insect. "She wants his blood so she can heal herself."

Gina looked at Mather, then at the insect. Mather gave her a dirty look in return.

"Right . . ." Gina wasn't accepting all I was telling her. Not that I was surprised. But she did seem to be playing along. After all, however surreal the situation, it would be obvious to anyone that something with serious conse-quences was about to take place.

238

"Look, it's not the pain I'm worried about," Mather said to the insect, a strange look on his face. "I just—" He seemed threatened by the Ganges Red, perhaps for the first time.

I must have your blood. It is the only way for me to regain my strength and fight Tien Thai. Now put down that weapon and GIVE ME YOUR BLOOD!

"No!" Mather remained defensive.

The insect was furious now. Gina took hold of my elbow and pulled softly, drawing me backward with her, away from Mather.

"Let me deal with the dragonfly," Mather said. "Then you can drain these two dry."

No! If you don't let me have your blood then I will take it by force—and then it really will hurt.

"No! You wouldn't." Mather was losing control of the situation now, and he knew it. "Not after all I've done for you!"

You did all I told you to do, nothing more.

"But there has to be another—"

Just then I heard the mosquito utter a shrill cry. It must have been louder in Mather's mind because he lowered the shotgun and raised his left hand to his forehead. He was clearly in great pain. "Stop! Stop! Why are you doing this to me?" He seemed now to be on the verge of tears.

The mosquito didn't relent; instead she continued her assault, clearly unwilling to end Mather's suffering until he gave in to her thirsty demand. Then, to my surprise, the hand fell away from his head, and he once again held the gun up in both hands, leveling it straight at my chest. I heard Gina gasp. Perspiration was saturating Mather's brow, his teeth were gritted and a barely audible whimpering could be heard, exposing the immense strain involved in fighting the insect's will.

"You!" Mather was talking to me now. "This is all your fault! You should be long dead." I could see his finger tense over the trigger. My body was frozen in shock. My tongue stuck to the roof of my mouth as I prepared for the inevitable impact.

Noooooooo! He's mine!

The mosquito flew at Mather, diving straight into his hair, no doubt seeking his scalp so she could plunge her feeding tube in. Mather danced about, screaming, and fired into the air, deafening us. He dropped the shotgun and started slapping at the insect with his hands.

"We need to get away from here fast." Gina stared in sheer amazement at the spectacle taking place some meters away.

"The tunnel," I replied. "I forgot about it. It's our best chance."

"Tunnel?"

"I think there might be a tunnel under the island. Soames showed me the entrance. I think . . . I think it's the only chance we have."

"Who?"

"I think it connects to the mainland somewhere."

"All right. How do we get there?"

"There's a trapdoor in the forest. I think I can remember the way there."

Gina's face fell. She didn't like the prospect of running off into the darkness of the trees. But we hardly had a choice. We were about to move when Mather finally detached the insect from his head, scooped up the shotgun and ran toward the building, the incensed mosquito in close pursuit. He rushed inside and immediately closed and bolted the door behind him. The Ganges Red changed course, headed round the side of the house and flew in through the smashed bedroom window.

"OK," I said to Gina, who now clung to my right arm for support. "Come on. Maybe they'll kill each other, maybe not. If not, then one of them is going to come after us. And whichever one it is, they'll want blood. Let's go."

I took her hand and led her to the path. Although it was dark, and much of the forest looked the same, I was pretty confident I could find my way to the hatch. Despite my tender ankle, we were able to make good progress. With the threat of murder still strong, maybe it's little wonder that I was still able to move fast despite my injuries. We stopped just where the forest began. From somewhere behind us we heard more breaking glass. Gina pushed the branches away from her, allowing some to fly back and hit me in the face.

"Ow!"

"Oh, sorry." She stopped to let me move ahead and lead the way. I soon became worried that I was getting us lost.

"Where now?" Gina looked around, seeing nothing but unfamiliar forest. I was about to admit defeat, when through the trees to our left I spotted a familiar rise in the ground.

"It should be straight ahead of us somewhere!" We continued forward, and a couple of minutes later broke into the larger clearing, in the middle of which was the trapdoor. I knelt down with some discomfort and grabbed the rope handle.

"Look," Gina said. I turned and saw she was pointing up into the night sky. There was a cloud of black smoke rising from the island and obscuring the pale moon above us. The research center.

"Clever," I said. "He gets you to take photographs for posterity, then burns the bodies."

"He hasn't got the photos," she said, patting her camera. "I have."

I gave her a grin. "Well, we can't do anything with those until we get off the island." I hoisted up the trapdoor, Gina bending to help me. We threw it back flat against the ground, disturbing the leaves.

I took to the ladder, which had been crudely fashioned from logs, and descended carefully, mindful of my wounded ankle. The tunnel could only have been about seven feet high. I could have jumped down from the forest floor if I'd had two healthy ankles. Nevertheless, I dropped off the ladder onto a soft, almost spongy mud floor which, even in the gloom, I could see was peppered with dead leaves and the odd puddle. There was a bad smell of age and damp that meant the tunnel had been around for quite a while.

"Pull the hatch down behind you," I called up to Gina.

"OK." I heard her try to grab it and pull it down. After a few moments she gave up. "I can't move it. It's stuck."

"All right, leave it—we haven't got time."

Seconds later Gina dropped to the floor behind me with a splash. Complete darkness swallowed us up. She blinked at me.

"Let's go." I started down the tunnel. After only a few steps I stopped. It was pitch-black and I hated the idea of tripping again. "I don't suppose you brought a flashlight with you?"

"No, I didn't," Gina replied.

"Ah, hell."

"Sorry."

"It's not your fault." Then I remembered. "Wait, your camera . . ."

"What about it?"

"The flash is working, isn't it?"

"Of course."

"Good, then we'll use the flash to light the way."

"Good idea." She raised the camera and moved ahead of me.

Gina led the way, lighting up the tunnel each time the flash warmed up. We made good time, and before long emerged into a large round chamber. Gina's flash was still working fine. I asked her to aim it at the walls. To my surprise, in the first flash I glimpsed what looked like a trapdoor. The flash went off again and we could both see that there was a hatch in the ceiling of the chamber over by the far wall, above a small set of steps that seemed to be carved out of the natural rock.

"It probably leads to the house or something," I said. "Let's just carry on."

Gina pointed the camera at the continuation of the tunnel to our right, and fired off another flash. As we were about to head into the opposite tunnel, the hatch was thrown open and a shaft of light penetrated the open chamber. I saw the barrel of a shotgun, and moaned.

"I can see you! Don't move or I'll kill you both!"

Gina swore; I just hung my head and sighed. *This will never be over,* I thought. *Never.*

He crept slowly down the steps, the gun never leaving his target. His hair was bedraggled, his face pale and haggard. A flashlight was tucked under one arm, allowing him to hold the gun with both hands. Like me, Mather had been through some pretty rough moments in the past few hours. He looked like a vampire, drained and deathly, as he dropped into the water with a splash.

"So, you thought you were out of here, eh? I'm afraid I can't allow any happy endings. In fact, the end is going to be particularly unpleasant for both of you."

"Where's the mosquito?" Gina fixed Mather with an evil stare.

"She is otherwise engaged right now. I'll deal with her later."

"I think *she's* going to be dealing with *you*," I said. "That's if she can handle the dragonfly."

"The dragonfly will also be taken care of, don't worry about that. Besides, if it were capable of doing anything, it would have done it by now."

"I wouldn't be too sure."

"You know nothing, Mr. Reeves. Absolutely nothing. It's a real shame that the operating theater is no more. I had some really exciting plans for you." He turned his attention to Gina. "I would have had an enlightening evening with this young lady too, if you hadn't so rudely interrupted us." He smiled. "No matter. Perhaps there are things I can do with this," he said, waving the shotgun, "that can provide some amusement. Now then," he went on, moving to the side of the steps. "Up we go."

We couldn't believe it. Just when we thought we'd been given a second chance at freedom, Mather had thwarted us again. Our luck seemed to have deserted us completely. We emerged into the living room of that hateful house. Mather ordered us to stand against the fireplace. There was no sign of the Ganges Red, but I figured that if the living room door and window were closed, there was no way it could get to us.

"Well now, who shall go first? The journalist or the photographer? I suppose the lady should go first, although as she's a photographer, she may appreciate the artistic splendor of death at close hand. Eh, Mr. Reeves?"

"Go to hell," Gina said.

"It'd be a short trip," I remarked. "But you've been

very sloppy over the past few hours. Pretty soon there'll be police officers all over this island."

"Well, yes, I realize that now. But they're not going to have an easy time of it. Once the Lady has calmed down I shall persuade her to stick to our original plan."

"Which is?"

"If they come . . . we kill them."

"All of them?" Gina looked incredulous.

"Well, as many as possible before the odds become too overwhelming. I think we'll be able to plough through a good many first, though—she with her fatal bite and me with my good friend here."

"Do you want me to state the obvious?" My eyebrows were raised in barely controlled disbelief.

"And what would that be?"

"You're mad," Gina said for me.

Mather laughed. "Oh, I see. Well, madness is subjective."

"Not in this case," I said.

"Yes, well, enough procrastination—I think we should get on with it."

Just then there came a curious sound from a dark corner of the room, the one to the left of the door. Gina and I looked in that direction. Mather, who was facing us, clearly wanted to look, but couldn't take his eyes from us. It had sounded to me like the high-pitched whine of a small motor, straining to turn something that was just too heavy for it. It continued for about fifteen seconds, then stopped. We then heard a soft vibrating sound, like rapidly beating wings. Mather was trying hard not to show it, but I could tell he was scared, quite possibly terrified. And he had very good reason to be. The sound had to come from one of two creatures, and Mather was on bad terms with both of them. He seemed to be shaking.

"You're in trouble now."

"Perhaps," Mather said. "But I'll deal with that when I've blown you into little bits." He raised the shotgun to eye level. I closed my eyes.

In what could have been my final seconds, I started praying fast and hard that something or someone would intervene and save us. Instead of a shotgun blast, there was an odd whizzing sound. Opening my eyes, I saw a small shape fly from the shadows like a sleek, silver dart and skate across Mather's balding scalp before disappearing back into the shadows. There was a chance that Mather could have pulled the trigger in a reflex action, but thankfully he just spun round, intending to face his attacker. He aimed the weapon at various places around the room, but couldn't find what he was looking for. Then, out of the corner of his eye, he spotted something and wheeled round to face the window. There it was.

Now that it was in the light I could see that the Yemen dragonfly was mainly gray in color, with the odd sparkle of silver. Its wings were huge and the head, with the large segmented eyes, seemed to radiate a sharpness, an intelligence. Mather clearly wasn't interested in examining the creature, as he quickly unloaded the shotgun at the window. Amazingly, the dragonfly was gone before the first pellets impacted on the glass. There was a wide, gaping hole in the window now, but no sign of the insect.

Mather cursed. "Damn! Where did it go?"

"I don't know, but you're a pretty lousy shot," Gina sneered. It was as though the shotgun didn't worry her in the slightest.

In response Mather pointed the weapon at her. "I don't always miss my targets, young lady."

"No," I insisted. "Please don't do it!"

"Of course"—he aimed at me again—"I forgot what I was doing for a moment. You were first in line, weren't you?" I was staring down the barrels of the shotgun once more.

"That's a double-barreled shotgun," Gina said. "So you've only got one shot left. I'll get you before you re-load."

"Oh, I don't think so. I've still got my dagger. Good-bye, Mr. Reeves. It really is a shame to waste you like this." He was adjusting his aim, perhaps for the last time, when the Ganges Red flew through the broken window and fastened itself to Mather's forehead before plunging its feeding tube directly into his right eyeball.

XVI: EXTERMINATION

The shotgun fired, blowing a large chunk of plaster out of the ceiling. Through the cloud that descended, Gina and I could see the ordeal unfold. Mather was waving his hands around in agony, while the mosquito made all sorts of wild noises. It sounded furious. As we watched, shocked and repulsed but too stunned to turn away, the flesh around Mather's eye bubbled and melted apart. Everything I'd heard was true. The Ganges Red really was as lethal as the legend had claimed. Soon the rest of his face was suffering from the effects of the toxic saliva. He kept on yelling his agonized protest, not letting up until he'd screamed himself hoarse. Steam rose from his head, adding an utterly detestable stench to a truly abominable sight. From the hissing skin below the eye, blood began to pool, landing on the carpet in small red circles.

The mosquito moved from Mather's forehead and attached itself to his neck, making considerably less noise now. It positioned itself comfortably, despite Mather's continuing frenzy, and proceeded to drain the blood directly from his jugular vein. Its wrinkled abdomen began to stretch and inflate as it gorged itself on the warm red liquid. As it grew, reclaiming its vitality, its wounds seemed to disappear. Glancing at the window, I could see that the dragonfly had returned. It was hovering in the hole created by the shotgun blast.

Gina had seen it too. "Come on," she whispered. "Let's leave them to it."

There was a huge explosion, which could only have come from the research center. Perhaps the generator's fuel tank had blown. Gina tugged at my arm, then pulled at the hatch. I helped her hoist it up and swing it over. Looking around, I saw Mather's flashlight lying on its side. After I'd grabbed it and switched it on, I couldn't help but take one last look at him. His face was already unrecognizable. There was a deep hole where his eye had been and parts of his forehead and right cheek had been reduced to a vile yellow substance. Perhaps it was my imagination playing tricks, but I could swear that in that instant his remaining eye turned to stare at me. I was about to scream when Gina grabbed my sleeve and pulled me down into the darkness of the tunnel, the trapdoor slamming behind me.

We waded across the subterranean chamber to the other side where the tunnel continued. I still had no idea where it headed, but it didn't really matter as long as it led away from the island. With the flashlight to illuminate our way, we made good progress. My limbs felt so heavy it was an effort to keep them responding to simple commands.

"Well," Gina said as we hurried along, "at least that maniac won't be bothering us again."

"It's not him I'm worried about."

"Well, unless that creature can eat through the trap-door in the forest, I think we'll be safe."

"But we didn't close that trapdoor."

"Oh, God, don't worry about it. We should concentrate on getting to the other end of this tunnel."

"If she knows about that entrance, and it's open, she can get down here."

"We haven't got time to worry about it. Besides, that dragonfly's still around, isn't it? It attacked the mosquito before, so maybe it's going to finish the job."

"Maybe. But we can't rely on it. The Ganges Red has proved herself to be pretty resilient—I can't believe what she just did to Mather."

"You're not feeling sorry for that freak, are you?"

"No, of course not. He got what he deserved." I could only imagine what was left of Mather by now. It was hard to wish that sort of death on anyone, but it was also difficult to believe he didn't deserve it. The pain in my ankle was getting worse and worse. I wanted to yell at Gina to slow down, to give me a break, but it wasn't an option. We simply had to get away from there as soon as we could, pain or no pain. Gina looked up and down the tunnel, a slight grimace of unease on her face.

"Why was that thing so interested in you, anyway? You weren't serious about it wanting your blood so it could become human . . . were you?"

"Yes. Although . . . I'm not sure now. Maybe it was the bang on the head that did it, after all."

"But you were convinced you could communicate with it. Mather talked to it as well."

"Yes, well, we're finally getting away, so who cares, right?"

"Right."

We maintained our speed for about half an hour before we heard something behind us. We stopped, looking at each other, our lips trembling. Gina pointed the flashlight back down the tunnel. The whining sound was growing in volume, but we could see nothing. We couldn't get away, let alone run, so we had to simply wait to see what happened. I saw it first. Its startling size was matched only by the dazzling red glow of its body. It seemed to be absorbing the light from the flashlight, becoming brighter, more intense.

"Oh, God," I said. I think we both knew that it was pointless to run, so we stood our ground. The mosquito would be upon us in seconds. Instead, Gina drew the flashlight back behind her head, preparing to strike. I didn't think it would do much good. One or both of us was going to die—I could feel it. The mosquito slowed down, then stopped to hover before us.

I have run out of patience. Give me what I want now . . . or suffer the same fate as Mather.

Gina gritted her teeth and glared at the creature. I stepped forward slightly, feeling a sudden surge of strength.

"All right. Take it." It was hard to say the words. The terror inside me had already fueled my imagination, bombarding my thoughts with all manner of horrific pictures.

But I saw no other option. If I continued to resist, I'd only push the Ganges Red into taking what she wanted by force.

Yes. That's it. It will be over before you know it. . . .

She flew forward again carefully, ready to move out of the way at the slightest hint of an attack.

"No, don't do it," Gina said, backing up slightly. And then she slipped on something, dropping the flashlight as she did so. In a flash the Ganges Red was upon me. She attached herself to my head and I went crazy.

What surprised me most was the heat she generated. It felt as if she were burning up. Even though I knew I'd done the only thing I could have, I was overwhelmed by the desire to throw her off me.

"Nooooooo!" Gina screamed somewhere behind me. "Get the hell off him!"

The mosquito crawled around my head, then without hesitation pierced the back of my neck, sucking with an awesome, tear-inducing power. This time I did scream.

I can't believe it's finally happening. Beloved . . .

Apart from the pain of the feeding tube breaking my skin and the sucking, there seemed to be nothing else. She hadn't injected her saliva, which came as both a relief and a shock. She must have been serious about keeping me alive. Incredibly, Gina seemed to be fading from my mind. The pain began to subside, as did the panic. Just as I was beginning to fall completely under the mosquito's welcoming influence, something roused me from my stupor. The tube was pulled out roughly, sending a spasm of pain down my spine. Then the creature flew off my head. I looked around, feeling tired, groggy, my vision slightly blurred, and saw Gina screaming at me.

". . . you hear me? Run!" She grabbed my hand and pulled me after her, neither of us particularly concerned about my weak ankle. I didn't know what condition the Ganges Red was in at that point, but I guessed she wasn't dead by the way Gina kept looking behind us and swearing. It was no great surprise to me when, soon afterward, I heard the whining sound again. My senses had cleared somewhat, and the full desperation of the situation had returned to me. We stopped, and with great dread turned to face our pursuer.

My blood had already wrought an extraordinary change upon her. Against comprehension, she had now grown to the size of a crow. And her size wasn't the only thing that had been altered. Her eyes were no longer segmented as they should be. They were white, cloudy. I thought I could see a tiny black dot like a pinprick in each of them, but it was hard to be sure. A dramatic transformation was without doubt now taking place. But could she really be turning into a woman? Despite what my eyes were seeing, the rational part of my brain was refusing to believe it.

She hovered and buzzed in front of us, perhaps deciding what to do, knowing she could take her time. The feeding tube looked twice as big as before: a long thick needle, cruelly pointed and still dripping. I felt the tender hole at the back of my neck. It was wet with blood, but there seemed to be no further damage. I looked across at Gina.

"Do something, for heaven's sake," she said.

"Like what?"

"Not you," she replied, turning to me. "That thing! Is it just going to hover there forever until we die of starvation?"

The mosquito's wings flapped out of time for a second. She was agitated, but she floated silently forward toward Gina, then up and above her, so that the tips of her wings were brushing the ceiling of the tunnel. Without warning she dived at Gina's head, stopping just short of her hair, then flew off again. This time I could hear her laughing.

Gina was shaken. She looked at me, trying not to show her fear.

"It's OK," I said, trying but failing to disguise the tremble in my voice. The mosquito just kept on laughing, bobbing up and down in merriment. I could see that the eyes were now definitely forming pupils. The sight was unsettling.

Yes.

The laughter had ceased.

I can look upon you with human eyes now. It is such a strange feeling. . . . I don't feel alien anymore, I feel like I'm coming home. It can't be long now. Soon I shall be as I was.

"And what then?" I was aware, as I spoke, of Gina turning to face me. She must have thought I was crazy or delirious to be talking to the thing again.

Then we will go far away from here. Somewhere new

where no one will find us and we can be alone for the rest of our lives.

"I told you, that's not going to happen."

I just need time to convince you. Once you've seen me as I really am, you will change your mind. You will love me as I love you. It won't be long now, I promise.

"I'm telling you! That won't happen. We're leaving this island. What you do is of no concern to me. Find someone else—anyone—but leave me out of it. I've already given you what you want. Why don't you just let us go?"

I thought you understood how I felt—the pain of desire? The doubt, the emptiness?

I looked at Gina. From the expression on her face it was clear that she wanted to know what was going on. I couldn't think of anything to say to her. Instead, I turned back to the Ganges Red.

"Yes, you're right. But you have to let her go."

The mosquito's buzzing grew louder. I had the feeling that she was upset now, and losing her patience.

She has corrupted your mind. She must die. Open your mind completely to me. Submit, and there will be no more pain. You deserve better than to slave under her tyranny. She'll control and rule you forever if you don't rid yourself of her now. Please . . . let me help you. . . .

"Don't touch her, or I swear—"

I won't harm her if she leaves now. Tell her to run and not look back. Once her influence has gone you will understand.

If it ensured Gina's safety, I was prepared to do what

the mosquito wanted. I had neither the time nor the strength to try to save myself as well. The insect had already drained much of my energy, and now my will was also starting to ebb.

"OK. But promise me you won't harm her. I'll do what you want if you let her go."

Of course I promise, my love. All I want is to make you happy.

"All right." I turned to Gina, who looked deeply concerned. Perhaps she had guessed what was going to happen. "Listen, you have to go—now. Just continue down the tunnel and get the hell out of here."

"You must be kidding. I'm not leaving you here with that!"

"There's no other option. Look, I'll be fine. She won't hurt me. You get away and go to the police. I have a feeling I won't be here when they arrive—but at least they'll find Mather. Maybe some of the bodies will have survived for them to identify."

"I'm not leaving you here."

"You have to!"

"Oh, no, I don't!"

"Listen." I grabbed her shoulders and looked into her eyes, so wide with fear. "If you stay here, we'll end up having to watch each other die. That's the truth of it. We can't kill this thing. We should be grateful she's allowed us this much mercy."

"I'd never forgive myself, Ash. I can't do it. I can't abandon you."

"Please. You have to, it's the only way I can protect you." I realized then that it was probably the last opportunity I'd ever have. I had to tell her. "I love you."

"What?"

"I've been in love with you since the day you started working at the magazine, and I can't bear the thought of never seeing you again. But look—just go, please. This is the wrong time for all this, I just . . . needed you to know."

"I . . ." Gina said nothing for some moments, then: "He really hit you hard with that shovel, didn't he?"

I smiled despite everything. "Go on, please," I said. "Before she changes her mind." I let go of her.

She looked at me for a long moment, then cast the mosquito a terrible glance. I expected her to utter some threat or curse. Instead, still gazing at the hovering menace, she spoke to me. "What you said just now—that's the nicest thing anyone's ever said to me." And with that, she turned and ran off. I watched her go; watched the cone of light from the flashlight get smaller and smaller. I was now alone with the monster, which was generating an awesome red light. There was a popping sound, and I saw that the mosquito's body had increased in size yet again. It really was an amazing sight. I would have been in awe if I hadn't been so consumed with loathing and fear.

Not long now. Rest. Sleep. I will wake you when it is time.

The temptation was pounding at me like a hammer.

I needed sleep badly. Nevertheless, I had a nagging doubt. She sounded agitated, and I had the feeling that she wanted me to sleep for another reason. I decided it was best to stay awake.

"So, what about Mather? Don't you regret killing him?"

Why would I regret it? He was of no more use to me. His thirst for murder and ability to attract victims were the only things that made his existence tolerable. The world is a better place without him.

"He fed you, kept you safe. I doubt there are many others who'd have done the same."

Perhaps. But ultimately, all he did was for his own personal gain. He cared about no one but himself.

"Are you sure? Are you sure he didn't care about you?"

It is not important. You should sleep. I am changing fast now. It will be time soon. You should conserve your energy.

"Why do you really want me to sleep?"

What?

"What don't you want me to see?"

The transformation will be ugly. . . .

"That's not it. You don't care if I'm repulsed by that. There's another reason."

There was another popping sound, and I saw that her feeding tube was beginning to retract. Some of her legs were also getting shorter, receding back into the body, which seemed to be growing all the while.

I cannot remain potent for much longer.

"Potent? You mean dangerous?"

Yes. Uhh!

She writhed and twisted in the air as part of her abdomen ballooned and stretched.

No more time. If you won't sleep . . . I have no choice. I didn't want you to see this. You must understand—to assure your love I have to remove all connections your heart has made. . . . I hope you will forgive me in time.

She managed to straighten herself out. I saw now that her eyes were almost human, the pupils large, black and surrounded by bright rings of green. In that instant, seconds old, they revealed a foul intent. She burst forward, right past me, and flew down the tunnel, as big as a raven now and clumsier than before, but still moving fast.

"Gina!" I screamed, breaking into a run. "She's coming!" I knew beyond a shadow of a doubt that I had no hope of catching up with the monster. Even if I could have reached Gina in time, there was no way of protecting her. The Ganges Red was far too big to just be swatted away. She would kill us both. But I ran anyway.

Gina had made good progress down the tunnel, despite her reluctance to leave me. Now she was moving faster, trying to put as much distance between her and the monster as possible. It was no use, though. From my position some distance away, I could see the glowing horror gaining on her, closing the distance with terrifying speed. The mosquito would be upon her in seconds. By the time I reached her, she'd already be dead. Just then, as I found despair finally claiming me, something flew past my right ear. It was no larger than a sparrow, but it moved with a deadly intent and a speed that let it cut through the air. It spoke three words, carefully deposited in its wake.

Don't give up!

I didn't. Instead, I surged forward with energy dredged from some unknown place, and thundered down the tunnel, regardless of the nightmare I was hurtling into.

I was able to see the Ganges Red land on the back of Gina's neck, the surprising weight causing her to stumble and fall to her knees. Then, before the mosquito had a chance to do anything more, the dragonfly hit her like a bullet, removing her from Gina's neck, along with a clump of hair. Gina screamed, and though her eyes were filling with tears, she was able to watch what unfolded. I finally reached her, and held her to me. The two forms were thrashing about in the water that had dripped over time from the lake above. The Ganges Red, her body warped and distended almost beyond recognition, was wrestling with the dragonfly, its smaller body attached to the mosquito's back, wings flapping like mad. We could only gaze in awe at the battle, praying that the smaller creature would win.

Gina put an arm round my waist. Despite the adrenaline surging through my body, my vision clouded over and I started to black out. Gina saw this and shook me awake.

"Hey! It's not over yet."

I concentrated on the Ganges Red and her determined enemy. This was a decisive fight that could yield only one survivor. And judging by the way things were going, the outcome we both prayed for seemed unlikely. The dragonfly had stunned its swollen opponent, and was repeatedly stabbing her with a small pointed horn on its head, causing her pink abdomen to rupture and bleed. Nevertheless, it seemed unworthy opposition. I was convinced it was only a matter of time before the Ganges Red retaliated with a killing blow.

"I have to do something," Gina said. She pulled me over to the wall. "Here—hold this." She gave me the flashlight. "Point it at them."

"Why—what are you going to do?"

"This is the only opportunity we have. And you're in no fit state." She started walking toward the brawling adversaries.

"No, don't go over there. Please."

"It's OK. Trust me." She moved purposefully across the wet floor and stopped some inches from the insects.

No!

It was the mosquito, and she sounded as angry as ever, though this time the anger was tinged with fear.

Keep her back! Keep her back!

The two insects then became separated on the wet tunnel floor. They both seemed either unwilling or incapable of getting airborne. The dragonfly appeared to have expended all its energy during its frenzied attack, while the Ganges Red, still growing, reared up on her two longest and strongest legs and let out what was no longer a buzzing but an almost human scream. She was preparing to charge, to deal the death blow. Then, as Gina stood there waiting for her opportunity, I heard the other voice. It was the dragonfly.

Now! Do it now!

"Now, Gina!"

She raised her left foot. The Ganges Red turned in her direction and froze. She looked ready to scream again, this time in terror, but she didn't get the chance. The shoe came down on her head, and suddenly the water around Gina's legs was dark with blood.

We stayed where we were for some time, our brains numbed. At some point I was able to make myself walk over and stand next to Gina. I put my arm round her waist. Looking down, I saw a number of red and black lumps lying in the thin layer of water. Blood had splashed the front of Gina's jeans and the wall opposite. I couldn't believe how much of it there was. Looking at her face, I could see that she was still coming to terms with all she'd seen. She was drawing deep breaths and staring down at what was left of the mosquito.

"Did you hear it?" The question seemed to have come from my lips before I had thought to ask it.

"What?"

"The dragonfly. Did you hear it speak?"

"I heard . . . I heard you," she said, turning to me. "That's all."

Together we both looked at our gray savior. I moved the flashlight beam so that it wasn't shining directly on it. It was hovering above the ground now, and appeared to be a lot healthier than it was some moments before. It turned round and silently flew back down the tunnel.

"Well," I said, smiling at Gina, "I guess it's not important."

"No. . . . Come on, let's get the hell out of this place."

"Good idea," I replied, but then Gina stopped abruptly and took hold of my arm. Her smile faded.

"What's wrong?"

"Can't you hear that?"

We stood still, listening. At first I could hear nothing but the drops of water from the ceiling. Then I began to make out the sound of tiny splashes, coming closer and closer.

"Oh, no," I said. "What now?"

We started to back away. Gina took the flashlight from my hand and pointed it down the tunnel in the direction of the sound.

"What is that?"

"I don't know." I shook my head. "And I don't want to know."

"Shh. Look!" I did, though I really didn't want to. "What the hell is that?"

I could see two small orbs of green in the dark, coming toward us. It didn't register at first, but then I realized. Laughing out loud, I dropped to my knees. My hands were outstretched and tears were emerging unimpeded from my eyes. As the little figure came plodding and splashing into view, I heard Gina gasp. He slowed down, meowed and climbed onto my knees, standing with his back legs on my left thigh, his front legs on my chest. He rubbed his nose against mine, then brushed his right cheek against my chin.

"Hello to you too," I said. "You've no idea how pleased I am to see you." Gina knelt down beside me and began stroking Mr. Hopkins's back.

When we had finished lavishing affection on him, I picked him up and we continued down the tunnel. We must have covered at least two miles before we reached the trapdoor. As we drew closer we could see a plank of wood set into the side of the tunnel, underneath the door. It was old, yellowed and damp, but the letters on it were still legible.

TRYST

Mr. Hopkins began purring, the sound oddly amplified by our confines.

"All that," Gina said, while I climbed the small ladder to push open the hatch. "That stuff back there. No one's going to believe it happened, are they? I'm not even sure I do."

Instinctively I climbed back down to the floor and took her hand in mine. To my great relief she smiled.

"Do you really care?" I squeezed her hand tighter. "We're both alive after all."

"Yes . . . But I still don't think I should have left the office today."

"I'm glad you did, though."

"Come on, let's go. Before something else comes down that tunnel."

Hours later, after the sun had reclaimed the sky, Gina and I found ourselves in a sparsely occupied train, heading back to London. I opened my tired eyes and looked around the otherwise empty carriage. A sound had awoken me. I thought I'd heard a buzzing, not unlike that of a large insect. I listened for a while, but could detect nothing other than the noise of the train as it rolled speedily through the countryside.

After we had given our statements to the local police, all hell had broken loose. We were still at the police station when the detectives arrived, and when our story had been confirmed and our details taken, we were allowed to leave, with the assurance that we would be interviewed again in the near future. All we cared about then was getting home and into a warm bed.

Before heading to the station, however, we had one last bit of business to take care of. After explaining my failure to show up last night to a rather bemused Annie Rocklyn, I asked if she wouldn't mind finding a home for Mr. Hopkins.

"Sir Anthony!" she exclaimed, darting from behind the counter to pick up the startled cat in her arms. "My word, where on earth did you find him? I thought I'd lost him long ago! Oh, you poor, poor puss. Mummy's missed you so much. Yes, she has."

We left the reunited couple to their celebrations and left the guest house.

Now, sitting in the train, I looked at the pretty girl sleeping next to me, using my arm as a pillow. Her shoulders rose and fell as she slept, and her contentment was infectious. I felt a great calm then, not just because it was all over, but because I'd got closer to her than I'd ever been.

I couldn't help pondering over what she'd said when we were climbing out of the tunnel. It was true that few, if any, people would believe our story. And I had a feeling that the more time that passed, the less I myself would believe it. Maybe it's part of time's great healing process, a way of ensuring that we don't go insane after the inexplicable events we're sometimes foolish enough to stumble into.

As I closed my eyes and let sleep welcome me into its arms once more, the only thing I was aware of, besides the endless drone of the train, was a very slight, almost imperceptible throbbing at the back of my neck.

EPILOGUE

An Lao Valley, Vietnam
2005

One minute Cam was tying cord around the broken branch of a mulberry tree, the next he was looking toward the spot where his wife, Long, had been sitting on a tree stump, sewing his tattered work shirt. And all he could see was a body, slumped on the ground.

He turned and ran to the spot where she lay, heaving her into his arms, calling her name over and over again in the hope that it might rouse her from the mysterious sleep that had overcome her. His efforts were to no avail. He checked for breath, for a pulse, but neither could be found.

How? How could his beloved, the only ray of sunshine in his life, have been taken from him so instantly, so unexpectedly, so silently?

He carried her body back to the hut and laid her down on the bed. Pacing around the chamber, panting, holding back tears that would surely consume him, he tried to think of something—anything—that could reverse what had happened. And then he remembered.

An old man lived in the mountains to the east of the small village. He rarely came down, and people rarely went up, but stories had circulated for decades of his powers. He was said to be as old as the mountains and wiser than any other man alive. The elders of the village swore that he was a genie, that he could heal, perhaps even restore life. It couldn't possibly be true, but Cam had to find out for sure. Life without Long just didn't bear thinking about.

For seven hours he carried his wife's body up the treacherous mountain path, until, late in the day, he arrived at the peak. It was colder up there and the path was almost overgrown with thorn bushes. Looking around, the wind bringing tears to his eyes, he spotted a small wooden building. He pushed through the harsh thorns, cutting himself numerous times, until at last he stood before the door of the hut.

The door was half open, but Cam could see only darkness inside. He was about to place Long's body on the ground before stepping inside, when a voice called out: "Stop! Do not come closer. I know why you are here, and I cannot help you."

"You—" Cam began, feeling the tears run from his eyes. "You cannot do anything?"

"What you ask means more than you can imagine. The dangers are immense."

"So you *can* do it?" Cam moved closer to the doorway, straining to see within, but making nothing of the dark shadows.

"I can . . . but—"

"You must!" Cam dropped to his knees. "Please, I will do anything, anything if you bring her back to me." He now started sobbing openly, staring into the hut in the hope that his earnest grief would spur the old man into acquiescing.

There was a pause, during which Cam's sobs and the howling wind were all that could be heard. Then: "Did she love you? Unconditionally?"

"Yes," Cam replied immediately, wiping his eyes. "We loved each other more than you can imagine."

"And was she content with her life? Was she never tempted to leave you for another? Another who could offer her more?"

"No!" The man was firm, almost angry. "Her only desire was to be with me. That and nothing more."

"Hmm," came the reply.

"I am going nowhere until you bring her back to me, old man. If you don't, I shall kill myself right now." Cam stared into the darkness, knowing the truth in his words would not be mistaken. "If I can't be with her in this world, I shall join her in the next."

There was another pause. For some minutes Cam knelt on the ground, wondering what would happen. Then he saw a face appear in the gloom of the hut. It was older than he could imagine. The skin was dry and horribly wrinkled, the hair thin and brittle. He had never seen a creature so old and frail.

"Very well, young man," the old man sighed, shifting uncomfortably. "Carry her inside. And bring one of those mighty thorns with you."

Dean Vincent Carter is a shadowy, fleeting character who works in the basement of Random House UK, sorting the mail. He claims to have seen so many dark and inexplicable things in his life that a career in horror writing was inescapable.

ACKNOWLEDGMENTS

On a research level I would like to acknowledge the book
Mosquito: The Story of Man's Deadliest Foe, by Andrew
Spielman and Michael D'Antonio, as a valuable source
of facts about the terrible insect itself. Any factual errors in
the novel, however, are mine alone. Aside from this and
numerous visits to the World Wide Web, the rest comes
from the depths of my imagination . . . God help you all!

I would like to thank everybody at Random House
Children's Books not only for publishing me, but also, along
with the folks at Transworld Publishers, for being valuable
colleagues and friends, always generous with praise,
support, and encouragement. I really do love you guys.

And most importantly, an overwhelming and ongoing
gratitude to a certain lady I met at a party once.
Charlie Sheppard: respected editor,
trusted friend, and true hero.
Thanks, Charlie.

—D. V. Carter, 2005